LIAM

A Brothers Ink Story

By
Nicole James

LIAM

BROTHERS INK
BOOK 3

By
Nicole James

Published by Nicole James

Cover Art by Viola Estrella
and
Mayhem Cover Creations
Photography by Ian Pettigrew
Models: Travis and Memphis Cadeau
Edited by CookieLynn Publishing Services

CHAPTER ONE

Liam stood at the Brothers Ink booth at the tattoo expo in LA. He couldn't take his eyes off the gorgeous tattoo model doing a photo shoot for the crowd. She was on a raised dais on a mock bed with a white fur throw under her. It was the perfect backdrop for the colorful ink that covered her sexy body. As the videographer filmed her, the feed was thrown up on a giant screen, like they do behind bands at concerts. She rolled around on the fur, and the entire event space had a perfect view. Her textbook pin-up vibe called out to every man in the room.

She was on her back; her bare legs extended in the air, crossed at the ankles, sexy platform shoes with sexier still straps wrapped around her smooth skin.

Her lips were painted bright red, her hair tied up in a fifties style bandana, ah la Rosie the Riveter, and she wore a fifties style two-piece bathing suit.

The cameraman filmed from over her head,

and she tilted her head back to look at him, her teeth coming out to nibble at her bottom lip. She rolled to her stomach arching her ass into the air with her arms stretched like a cat.

Jesus Christ, the woman was sex on a stick. Every man in the place probably had a hard-on for her.

She was selling a pin-up calendar at the event, and they were going fast, even at thirty bucks a pop. Liam could see why. He couldn't tear his eyes from her. What he wouldn't give to run his hands over her skin and trace every tattoo she had with his tongue. Hell, he'd even settle for putting some ink of his own on her gorgeous body.

"She's hot, isn't she?"

Liam glanced over at his brother, Rory. "Hot as hell." His eyes turned back to the screen. "I'd love to lay ink on her, wouldn't you?"

"Hell, yeah. Why don't you go ask her? It'd be an icebreaker, anyway, even if she weren't interested in more ink."

Liam drained the last of the bottle of water in his hand and tossed it in the trash. "I'm going to take a walk around the hall… check out our competition. You got the booth covered?"

"Yeah, man, go on. But remember I've got to catch

a flight for that gig tonight in Seattle, so we need to tear down the booth as soon as the expo closes."

"I'll be back by then."

Liam strolled around the exhibit hall, greeting old friends in the business he'd known for years and shooting the shit. He also took the time to say hello to many newcomers and check out their artistry. He believed in being supportive and welcoming with a mentoring spirit, as long as the artists and shops followed good industry practices. Over the years, he'd seen many players come and go in this business, some whose flame of fame would flare up brightly only to burn out within a few years because they didn't maintain those industry standards. It was truly a tough business to succeed in, especially long-term.

He was thankful every day for the success Brothers Ink had attained, and he knew most of the credit went to his older brother, Jameson. He'd started the business as a way to support his three younger brothers after their parents were killed in a car accident. Liam would be forever grateful that Jameson had stepped up to the task, rather than let them all be split apart into different foster homes.

Not only had Jameson taken care of them, he'd

given them all a profession, and it was one Liam loved. He was in his element here at the expo. He loved meeting the fans and rubbing elbows with his contemporaries. To some extent, it was like a reunion for him.

"Hey, Liam, how are you man?" An artist with a long braid stepped around to take his hand and pull him in for a backslapping hug.

"Carter," Liam returned the embrace. "How're things in Vegas?"

"Great. When are you going to make the trip? I'll show you the town."

"The Vegas Strip isn't really my thing. I'm more of the outdoors kind."

"You gonna be at the Miami show in the fall?"

"I don't know. Jameson makes all the arrangements; I just show up."

Carter laughed. "I hear ya, man."

"I've got to get back to the booth. We need to start tearing down soon. Rory's got a flight he needs to catch."

"Where's he off to?"

"Seattle. His band, Convicted Chrome, is playing tonight."

"How's that going for him?"

"They're good. Have you seen 'em play yet?"

"Haven't had a chance. They got anything on the radio yet?"

"Nah, they're still waiting for their big break. Take it easy, man!"

"You, too." After making his way back around, he returned to the booth. Rory was taking a photo with a couple of giggling girls, his long dark hair standing out between the two blondes pressed to his sides.

Liam began breaking down the booth while Rory took pictures and signed autographs. Some even knew him from Convicted Chrome. Liam gave him the time and took down the shop's standing banner and stowed it in its bag.

"Did you go talk to her?"

Liam looked up to see Rory now standing at the table alone. "Who?"

Rory huffed out a laugh. "The tattoo model, that's who. Moron."

"Nah."

"Afraid you'd get shot down?"

"Fuck off."

A female artist from another booth approached the table. "Rory, can I get a selfie with you?"

"Sure, Vonda." He leaned across the table, tucked his long hair behind one ear and smiled his megawatt smile, pressing his cheek to hers. She pulled back, and he lifted his chin. "Text me a copy, babe."

She waved goodbye and walked off.

Liam shook his head.

"What?" Rory asked.

"You draw 'em like flies."

"I can't help it. I got all the good looks in the family."

Liam chuckled and shoved the last of their gear in a duffle bag. "Tell Jameson's legions of followers that one."

Rory rolled his eyes then nodded toward the end of the hall. "They're packing up. She'll be gone soon."

"I realize that."

"For once in your life, brother, take a damn risk."

"What are you talking about? I take risks all the damn time. I went with you just last spring to climb Medicine Man. Got all the way to the top, didn't I?"

"Yeah, I guess Medicine Man is a good climb for a beginner like you," Rory teased.

"Fuck off."

"I'm not talking about rock climbing, dumbass, I'm talking about taking an emotional risk."

"What the fuck is an emotional risk?"

"You always settle for the ones that come on to you instead of going after the ones you're really interested in." He lifted his chin toward the end of the hall. "Like Velvet Jones."

"I don't do that."

"Yeah, you do, bro. All the time. Opportunity's staring you in the face, but if I know you, you're too afraid you'll get burned."

"Don't you have a flight to catch?"

"Plane leaves in two hours."

"What time does your band take the stage?"

"Nine tonight. Why don't you come?"

"You know I have to drive the truck full of all this shit back to Colorado."

"Sucks for you."

"Yeah, so you should be nice to me."

Rory's lips split into a devilish grin. "Maybe I'll go see if I can get Velvet to sign one of those calendars for you. I'll have her make it out to my ugly older brother."

"Gee, thanks."

***

An hour after the expo closed, Velvet and her photographer sat at the hotel bar. It was a nice place, sleekly decorated and dimly lit.

Velvet lifted her lemon drop martini. "To us."

Aaron lifted his Scotch. "To you, beautiful."

They toasted, and Velvet gave him a small smile as she licked the sugary rim of her drink. "I can't believe we sold over a thousand copies of the calendar this weekend."

"I can. The men loved you. Hell, at one point the line for you to sign them was down the entire aisle. I was afraid we were going to run out of copies."

"I never would have believed it. I thought you were crazy for bringing all those cartons."

"We completely sold out this weekend."

"There's another tattoo expo in New York coming up. Maybe we can hit that one?" she suggested.

He set his glass down and ran his finger around the rim. "Not sure I can get them printed in time, and it's probably too late to get a booth."

Velvet frowned. Aaron was usually so positive and enthusiastic about the opportunities for them. It just wasn't like him, but she nodded. "Okay. Maybe Miami or—"

He cut her off. "Yeah, sure. We'll see. Let's talk about that tomorrow."

"All right."

He downed what was left of his drink. "I need to call Angie. She's left me several messages. She'll be excited to know how the event went." He stood, digging in his wallet and throwing some bills on the bar. "If you don't mind, I think I'll call her from my room."

Velvet started to push her drink away.

"No, honey. You stay. Enjoy your drink. I'll call you first thing in the morning; we'll meet up for breakfast and make some plans for the future, then get some good shots in with the morning light." He hugged her, then pulled away, his hands on her upper arms,. "You did good, kid."

"*We* did. I couldn't have done it without your beautiful photography."

He chucked her chin and then walked out.

Velvet turned back to the bar and lifted her glass. A bluesy song was playing, and she took a moment to savor her success. She stared at the bottles lit-up in an amber glow behind the bar. With the money they'd earned this weekend, she was that much closer to her dream. She was finally making enough money to do something she'd wanted to for years. She'd longed her whole life to be able to have her future dependent on only herself, to have her success or failure rely solely on her own shoulders, not be at the whim of someone else. She wanted to be her own boss.

She didn't want much. She didn't need fame or wealth. She just wanted a little piece of happiness, and in her eyes that was something as far from the world she found herself in as one could imagine. Looking at her ink, one would never guess what her real dream was. She loved the tattoo world and the people she'd met in it, but it hadn't been her dream in life to be where she now found herself—a tattoo model. It was just a forced circumstance that had become a means to an end. What she wanted was as far from this as she could get.

She wanted a simple, cute little vintage coffee shop. She dreamed of lining shelves with books of all kinds. She dreamed of it being a place where people loved to come and spend time, where the community gathered and where all were accepted. She'd decorate it up big for holidays, and she'd definitely have a corner filled with children's books—something she'd never had as a child—and maybe even a colorful rug for them to lay on the floor and read while their parents sipped on delicious coffee drinks. That was her dream, and now with the earnings she'd split with Aaron on the calendar sales, she was almost able to have it. She was so close she could taste it.

She'd even found a location, and the landlord had given her until Tuesday to put the deposit down on the lease.

Someone slipped onto the barstool that Aaron had vacated, and the bartender approached, tossing a coaster down on the bar. "What can I get you?"

A deep male voice replied, "Bourbon. And get the lady another."

She turned to thank the man, but froze when she saw him.

Her stomach dropped, and she heard a roaring in her ears as the panic rushed through her. She said a quick prayer in her head that he didn't recognize her as the fifteen-year-old kid he'd once tattooed.

***

Liam glanced over at the beauty he'd been drooling over during the convention. He couldn't believe his luck when he walked in the bar.

His eyes took in the black pants that hugged her long legs, the high-heeled sandals, and the skimpy red top with skinny little straps that displayed all her colorful ink. She was stunning.

Here was his chance to take that risk Rory had berated him about. Maybe Rory was right. Maybe he needed to be more open to opportunity and quit worrying about getting burned.

"Hey." He greeted her with a smile.

"Hey."

"Nice ink." Shit, could he be more cliché?

"Thank you. You, too." Her eyes moved over the exposed ink at his neck and rolled up sleeves.

"I saw your line today. Your hand must be exhausted from autographing so many calendars." God, he sounded like such an idiot, like he'd never hit on a beautiful woman in his life. He wouldn't be surprised if she rolled her eyes and turned a cold shoulder on him. But, thankfully, the pick-up gods were smiling down on him. Instead of blowing him off, she grinned and flexed her hand.

"I'm recovering and this is helping." She lifted her drink and took a sip.

I bet it is. A pretty drink for a pretty lady. Does it taste as good as it looks?" What he really wondered was did *she* taste as good as she looked. By the tug at the corner of her mouth, she got the innuendo.

"Absolutely."

"Looks delicious."

She lifted her chin to his drink. "I'm sure there's something to be said for Bourbon straight up. It's such a manly drink, isn't it?"

He huffed out a laugh. "Well, I'm a man, so, yeah."

She seemed to relax and even giggled. It was a soft melodic sound that drew him further under her spell. "Yes, you definitely are, handsome."

Was she flirting with him? He extended his hand. "Liam."

She hesitated a moment, then took it. "Velvet."

"That's a unique name."

"I'm a unique woman."

"No argument here."

***

Fifty-four minutes later he was pulling her through the door to his room and falling onto the king-size bed. They rolled around on the white goose-down duvet cover, tossing articles of clothing to the floor piece by piece.

She climbed on top of him and began unbuttoning his shirt. His palms smoothed up her thighs while he let her undress him. She tugged the tails out of his jeans and went to work on his belt buckle. When it was open, he sat up and captured her mouth with his while he tugged her shirt over her head and tossed it to the floor.

Her bra was see-through lace and with a snap of his fingers he unhooked it and pulled it down her arms. Her gorgeous breasts popped free into his waiting hands. He squeezed them and brought one, then the other, to his waiting mouth.

She arched her back when he closed over her nipple and sucked hard. Her moan was music to his ears. He squeezed and sucked and played until she was writhing against his cock.

She dragged her sweet pussy against him, getting off on it. He had no problem with that; he loved that she took her pleasure, but it was torture for him.

He grabbed her face with his hands and latched his mouth to hers, sweeping his tongue inside. Her lips were soft and pliant, and she tilted her head back, giving him all the access he wanted. He stroked one hand down her long delicate neck and threaded his fingers into the hair at her nape. He held her head in position while he thoroughly kissed her.

Finally, in need of breath, he lifted his mouth from hers. "Goddamn, I've wanted to taste you from the moment I saw you rolling around on that white fur.

You were so hot, sweetness. God, I'd love to see you rolling around on it topless, that soft fur tickling these pretty pink nipples. Would you like that, baby? Would that turn you on?"

"If it turned you on to watch me, I'd do it."

"Hell, then I'll buy a white fur rug."

"The way you talk."

His hands drifted down to cup her lush ass, controlling her writhing motions and applying more pressure. "You like that?"

"Oh, God, yes."

"It's fucking torture. I want inside you so bad, lady."

He rolled her until her back was flat on the bed. Then he moved up to his knees and worked the fastening of her pants. He stood at the foot of the bed and slipped her sexy as sin strappy little sandals off her feet, noting the pink polished toes and the trailing vine that was tattooed around one ankle. He slowly pulled her pants off, revealing what had to be God's gift to mankind. Her long legs were perfectly shaped, and his eyes trailed up them. Colorful ink ran up either thigh and over the gorgeous curves of her hips. His eyes stalled at the juncture of those beautiful thighs. A scrap of red lace that matched the bra he'd already tossed aside was all that covered her from his gaze. The see-through lace gave him a tantalizing glimpse of her delectable pussy. "You gonna let me taste that, Velvet?"

Her eyes were dark and shining, and her lips parted. She nodded, giving him the sweetest gift she had, and he wasn't taking that gift for granted. He wanted her to know how honored he felt; he wanted her to feel worshipped. He wanted her to remember every moment of this night, their first night together, but if he had anything to say about it, definitely not their last.

He dropped to his knees and pulled her toward him, spreading her thighs to accommodate his broad shoulders. "I want you to enjoy every second of our time together."

The pulse in her neck quickened at his words, and her breathing picked up.

He ran his palms up the inside of her thighs, his touch soft but firm, stopping just short of his goal and dragging the moment out until the anticipation made her squirm.

"Liam, please."

At the first stroke of his thumbs over her pussy, she jerked.

"Easy, sweetness. I'm only going to give you pleasure." He brushed the pads of his thumbs over her again, and then he dipped his head and inhaled her scent. It filled his nostrils and went straight to the primal part of his brain. He wanted her more than any woman he'd ever been with.

She sucked in a breath and lifted her hips. "Please."

He gave her what she wanted and licked her softly… slowly with the flat of his tongue.

Her fingers threaded into his hair and tried to pull him closer, but he was having none of it. She was a delectable treat, and he was determined to take his time savoring her. He grabbed her wrists and pinned them to the bed by her hips.

That had her writhing even more. "Oh, God, Liam."

"We go at my pace. I want to take my time, and you're going to let me, yeah?"

She stared down at him; her passion-glazed pupils dilated. "Yes. Yes. I'll give you whatever you want."

He licked her again and again, watching her belly tremble with the need he was building in her. She tugged on her wrists, but he held them tighter.

If she'd asked him to release her, he would have immediately, but she didn't.

She struggled to move, to bring her pussy to his mouth, but he held her thighs pinned beneath his muscular arms. He gave her just enough room to move an inch and barely lift to his waiting mouth. "Work for it, baby."

Her pussy coated with a new rush of wetness. This time, Liam was the one who gave in.

"Oh, yeah, baby. I love seeing that." He dipped his head and lapped and sucked and finally worked his way up to her clit. He gave it all the attention it deserved until she thrashed on the bed; her head flung back, and she begged him not to stop.

He gave her a wicked smile. "I have no intention of stopping anytime soon. I could feast on this sweet pussy all night long and never get tired of it."

True to his word, he kept on and on, stroke after stroke until she exploded in orgasm.

Her chest heaved, but he wasn't ready to give her a break just yet. He released one wrist and sank two fingers into her slick pussy, searching out her g-spot. Her hips jerked, and he knew he'd found it. "Bingo."

She stared down at him, her breasts slick with sweat. "Oh, God. I can't."

He kissed her inner thigh. "Yeah, you can, baby girl. I'll show you."

He worked her g-spot rapidly and gently stimulated her clit with soft circles. She writhed and squirmed, panting hard.

Liam spread one big palm over the trembling skin of her belly and applied pressure, keeping her pelvis pinned to the bed while he stroked her clit and g-spot. Wave after wave of release coated his fingers.

She lifted her head to watch, and Jesus Christ, she was the hottest thing he'd ever seen.

He could feel her clenching around his fingers. He wanted her to remember this night, like he knew he would remember the sight of her rolling around on that white fur forever.

He kept at her until her head dropped back, and she arched, her mouth dropping open. He took that moment to press down on her belly and up with the two fingers inside her, and she detonated, moaning loudly as she came hard.

She panted heavily, her body trembling. "Please, no more."

He gently withdrew his fingers but kept his thumb moving in soft slick circles as she floated back down. Then he lapped her clean.

He put a fist to the mattress and hovered over her body, taking her mouth with his. She moaned, her hands coming up to lightly touch his ribs.

He broke the kiss to look at her flushed face. Then he moved back off the end of the bed, stripping down. He pulled a condom packet from his pocket and tossed it on the bed, then dropped his jeans to the floor.

His eyes remained locked on hers, but her pretty blues dropped to his cock. He took it in his hand, giving it a stroke. It was already rock hard.

"You're the hottest woman I've ever seen, Velvet."

***

Velvet was used to men looking at her with lust in their eyes, but the way Liam looked at her now was different. His warm brown eyes were sincere, his words genuine.

She could only give him tonight, but she had a feeling he would never be satisfied with only one night. She knew she should have never even risked this much, but with this man, like no other, she couldn't fight the pull. It was like he was her one true mate, and she was incapable of denying him.

God, those unspoken thoughts would sound crazy if she dared speak them. She knew better than anyone that reality was nothing romantic. There were no soul mates.

But, Lord, with just a look, he was making her feel things she shouldn't dare let herself feel. A moment before she'd let herself forget everything but the feel of his warm mouth on her pussy.

As he stood there, her eyes moved over his muscular body, taking in all the tattoos she'd only ever wondered about. Now she could see every inch of them, and they were beautiful. Colorful masculine designs made him that much more attractive in her eyes, that much more dangerous; they accentuated every muscle group that corded his stunning body.

She couldn't help but lick her lips in anticipation of having that big masculine body on top of her. As if he read her thoughts, his mouth twisted into a half smile revealing pearly teeth. His eyes darkened, traveling over every inch of her, branding her with possession, before returning to her eyes, and she suddenly found it hard to breathe. She'd never in her life reacted to a man this way.

The vein in his neck pulsed, and a muscle in his jaw tightened. His eyes stalled on her bare pussy, and she squirmed in anticipation. That was all the invitation he needed. A predatory gleam was in his eyes when they flashed to hers. He leaned down, a fist in the bed and kissed his way up her body.

Desire shot through her veins with the tingle of his lips trailing across her sensitive skin. When he got to her breasts, he sucked and toyed with them at his leisure. His warm body settled, pinning her to the mattress.

His hard cock pressed against her thigh, and she swore she could feel it pulsing between them.

He released her nipple and took her mouth for one long kiss. "I need you," he breathed.

She nodded, even as he was already moving between her thighs, spreading her wide to accommodate his body.

He paused only long enough to tear open the condom packet and slip it on, and she felt pinned like a butterfly, helpless to do anything but take what he was giving. He dropped a hand to her breast and squeezed, his mouth sucking on her nipple. He dragged his touch down her belly, guiding his cock to her opening. He swirled the head in her wetness and then sank deep in one deep thrust.

Her head fell back and her mouth dropped open as

she gasped in a breath at suddenly being filled. He gripped her ass and held her firmly while he eased in and out, setting the pace and giving her every inch of him.

She couldn't help but clench down around him, and when she did, he emitted a growl from deep in his chest and picked up his pace until he was driving into her.

He lifted his weight off her, slipping a hand between them and strumming her clit. He dipped his head, murmuring hot words of sex into her ear until she couldn't think of anything but the sensations soaring through her. She moaned his name.

"You're fucking beautiful, Velvet. " His hand fisted in her hair. "It's never been this good with anyone else before. I feel it. Tell me you feel it, too."

She nodded, unable to deny it. "Yes, I feel it."

He kissed her softly at first, and then with more urgency. He trailed his lips down her neck, to her nipples, where he latched on hard until she tightened her legs around him and exploded in another orgasm.

He followed in a few more strokes, spearing into her and shouting his release.

CHAPTER TWO

Twelve hours later…

Velvet stared down at the gorgeous tattooed man lying among the white hotel sheets. They'd spent an incredible night together. He'd been her secret crush for years, and when the opportunity to spend the night with him presented itself, she'd jumped at the chance.

They'd shared an amazing connection, something she'd never felt before with any other man. And he'd felt it, too. He'd admitted as much last night.

Her gaze skated over his chest, where she'd cuddled against him when they'd both finally fell into an exhausted sleep as dawn approached. God, how she longed to lie back down beside him and take him in her arms. But as her eyes moved lovingly over his muscled inked body, fear flooded through her. She couldn't risk him finding out the truth. If he ever found out her secret, he'd look at her with different eyes, and he'd come to hate her, and that she couldn't bear.

So she did the only thing she could. She forced herself to slip out of his hotel room without saying goodbye, without so much as leaving a note. Of course she couldn't have left one if she wanted—and that was another secret she kept guarded. She couldn't read and could only write enough to sign her name.

She turned her back on what might be the only opportunity she had for any kind of relationship with the one man who had ever made her feel something, and that was why walking out that door was so incredibly hard.

The door quietly latched as she slunk out, and the feelings of regret overwhelmed her. She pressed her forehead to the door, and as her chest tightened, she allowed a single tear to fall. Finally straightening, she took a deep breath and walked down the hall. Stepping onto the elevator, she stared at the doors as they slid closed, and she couldn't help the hope that flared inside her that maybe last night would be as ingrained in his memory as she knew it would be in hers.

Yes, perhaps he would remember her. After all, she'd heard what men said about her... *Velvet – Nobody forgets Velvet.*

She took out her phone as she crossed the lobby

and dialed Aaron. He'd talked about meeting for breakfast and then doing a shoot with the city skyline as a backdrop, but she hadn't heard from him, and they'd have to be quick if they wanted to use the morning light.

He didn't pick up, and she frowned when a recording came on saying the subscriber was not available. *What the hell?*

She stood at the window and redialed, her gaze darting around the parking lot. As she listened to the message repeat again, her eyes locked on a figure, and her mouth fell open. Pulling the phone from her ear, she stared in disbelief. Aaron was across the parking lot, throwing a suitcase into the trunk of his car. Slamming it, he slid quickly behind the wheel.

What the fuck? Where the hell was he going? Was he leaving her here? They hadn't even split the money from yesterday's sales yet!

She dashed out the glass doors and ran after his car as he sped off the lot. "Aaron!" He didn't stop; he didn't even slow down.

He glanced at her as he flew past, the car accelerating. She stomped her foot. *Oh. My. God! That jerk!* He'd taken off with all the money! And he was her ride! She was left high and dry in LA.

"No, no, no! This cannot be happening. It has to be a mistake." She frantically dialed his number over and over but got the same message.

"You son-of-a-bitch!" she screamed into the air, her body going stiff with her rage.

When she calmed down enough to function, she dialed her best friend. "Chloe?" she whispered, her voice shaky.

"Velvet? What's wrong?"

"Aaron just took off on me... with all the money we made!"

"Are you shitting me?"

"I wish I was."

"Oh, baby, I'm so sorry."

"I can't believe this is happening. I had such big plans and everything hinged on that money. It was everything to me. My means of finally being able to break free of my family."

"Oh, Velvet. He took all of it?"

"We made over thirty grand."

"Wow! And he left you with nothing?"

"Yep. We were supposed to do another shoot this morning and split the money then. I can't believe I let this happen. I can't believe I trusted him."

"I'm so sorry, babe. I tried to warn you. In this

business you can't trust anybody. I've told you before, you're too nice."

"I thought he was different. I thought we were in this together."

"You deserve so much better, honey."

Velvet fought to swallow down the heartache. Every word her friend spoke was true. She did deserve better, and she needed to stop letting people use her. The funny thing was, she thought she already had. She believed she was really turning her life around. Everything had been looking up. She'd had big plans. And now? Now she didn't even have a ride.

"So what about that lease on that shop you were supposed to sign?"

"I won't be able to if I don't have the money Aaron stole."

"Well, you know you can keep staying with me for as long as you need."

"I hate to impose on you. You've already let me stay for longer than I planned."

"Honey, you're not even here half the time. It's no problem."

"This isn't how it was supposed to be. I was supposed to sign that lease and finally be able to make my dreams come true."

"I know, honey. Do you need me to come get you?"

"Um, maybe." She bit her lip, knowing her friend was hours up the coast. Her cell buzzed with an incoming call. "Hold on a second. Maybe that's him." She took the second call. "Aaron?"

"Nope, Kitty-Kat. It's your big brother."

Her shoulders slumped. "Vano."

"I was just driving through LA and heard you were at the big expo this weekend. You still in town?"

"Yes. Why?"

"Just thought we could get together for a cup of coffee or a beer. Haven't seen you in months."

"Hold on a second." She flipped back to Chloe. "It's Vano."

"Your brother?"

"Yep. Says he's in town. I can get a ride from him."

"I thought your goal was to disassociate with your family. You know they always suck you into their bullshit."

"I know, but what choice do I have? Anyway, I'll call you later."

"You sure you don't want me to come get you?"

"You're hours away. He's right here. It only makes sense."

"Do not let him pull you into any of his schemes."

"I won't. I've got to go before he hangs up."

"Okay, honey, but remember I'm always here for you."

"I know, babe, and I love you for it."

She chuckled. "Of course you do, I'm very loveable. But seriously, call me tomorrow or I'll hunt you down."

"I will. I promise." Velvet switched back to the call from her brother. "Hey. Sorry, I had another call."

"So, where are you?"

Velvet bit her lip, hoping she wouldn't regret this. "The Excelsior."

CHAPTER THREE

The AC kicked on and a cool breeze blew over the skin of Liam's back. He twisted his head, pulling the adjacent pillow under his face. Memories of last night flooded his brain as he sucked in the scent of Velvet's perfume on the hotel linen. He pushed up off his chest and scanned the room. Dim light filtered through the slit in the drapes.

"Velvet?"

The bathroom was dark.

He sat up quickly, scanning the floor and chair for her clothing, shoes, and purse. Nothing. She was gone.

His chest tightened with the ache of losing her. He didn't even have her number. He'd thought there'd be time for that this morning. He'd never imagined she'd sneak out on him.

Things last night had been good. Better than good—they'd been phenomenal. The two of them had clicked, intellectually and physically. Liam had never been one to believe in soul mates but something about her drew him in and made him feel like he'd found his other half.

Apparently, it was all one-sided. Although, last night, when he was on top of her, moving slowly in and out of her and staring into her gorgeous, expressive eyes, he could have sworn she was as connected as he had felt.

Jerking the sheet away, he strode naked to the window and pulled the curtain aside. He scanned the parking lot, not that he expected to see her. His hand closed in a fist around the fabric of the curtain. Damn it, the little minx could have at least said goodbye or…

His head swiveled to the far nightstand, scanning for a note and landing on the hotel notepad and pen.

His jaw tightened when he saw it was blank.

He stared out the window again, wondering at all that could have been and aching at the loss of it.

His phone rang, and he twisted to dig it out of the hip pocket of his jeans that lay on the floor by the bed. Hope flooded him once again that maybe it was her calling.

He stared at the screen.

Jameson.

He put the phone to his ear, taking the call. "Yeah

man?"

"What time are you leaving?"

"Noon."

"How'd the show go?"

"All right."

"Everything okay, brother?" Jameson had always been able to read him like a book.

"Yeah. Everything's fine."

There was silence on the other end. His older brother didn't buy his lie. "We'll talk when you get back."

"Yep."

Liam disconnected and tossed the phone on the bed. He slid his jeans on and again moved to the window. He leaned his palm on the frame and stared out at the traffic and the morning sun rising in the distance. He was different today. Last night had left an indelible mark on him. He stared at the horizon, but all he could see was Velvet's sparkling eyes. All he could hear was her soft laughter. All he could taste was her sweet kiss.

And now she was gone.

Goddamn.

***

"Sounds like you're in a bit of a predicament."

Velvet sat across the booth from her brother, slowly stirring her coffee. "You could say that."

Vano was well dressed, as usual, in a pair of expensive jeans, a nice button down, and his dark hair slicked back without a lock out of place. He grinned his Cheshire cat grin. "The best thing for you to do is come back home with me."

Velvet let out a huff. "Home? Where's home this week?"

"Grand Junction. I've opened up a shop. I could really use some help."

"A shop? Doing what?" She really wasn't interested in the answer; her brain was still stalled back on the location. Suddenly she felt light-headed.

"Don't be obtuse. A tattoo shop."

"A tattoo shop?" That drew her from her trance. "You tried that once. You hated it."

"I didn't hate it. I just had other opportunities come up."

She took a sip of her coffee cup and set it back in the saucer. "You were shit at it."

"Gee, thanks." He leaned his folded arms on the table.

"Sorry, but you know it's true."

"Whatever." He met her eyes. "Well, are you in?"

She looked away. "I don't know."

"I've got some artists working for me now. The place is doing pretty well."

Her gaze snapped back to his. "What do you need me for then?"

"You'd be a big draw for business, and I could use a hand. You got a better offer right now?"

Velvet drew in a deep breath and scanned the restaurant, her eyes going to the street beyond the window. She flipped the spoon on the table over and over. Vano would suck her right back into whatever shit he was doing. She knew it, and yet, what choice did she have? She was flat broke. No place to live and no job. Perhaps she could stand it long enough to get some modeling jobs lined up. Or maybe she could get another calendar put together. But Grand Junction was where Brothers Ink was located. What if she ran into Liam again? Perhaps it wouldn't be too hard to lay low. Surely she could avoid him for a few weeks.

Hell, she couldn't lie to herself; she'd want to catch a glimpse of him, at least from a distance.

"Velvet?"

Her brother's voice broke into her thoughts, and she turned back to him. "All right.

Temporarily."

"Suit yourself." The smile on her Vano's face betrayed the fact that he thought he'd succeeded in getting her back under his thumb.

If he thought she was going to be as easily manipulated as she'd been by her family in the past, he had a rude awakening coming. She'd been making her way on her own for years now, and although they constantly tried to suck her in, she swore her time with them would be short.

She had dreams in life, and she was determined somehow to make them happen. Being sucked into their bullshit was not part of her plan.

CHAPTER FOUR

Liam's mind wandered as he cleaned his tattoo station. He operated on autopilot a lot these days since he returned to town.

"So, how did the expo go?" Maxwell wiped down the chair at his station, his gloved hand running over the seat and armrests.

Liam pulled his gloves off with a snap and tossed them in the bio trashcan. "Good. Lot of people." Talking about it was the last thing he wanted to do.

Max gestured to the calendar Liam had recently stuck up on his mirror, the one Rory had gotten for him. "Was *she* there?"

Liam glanced up and reluctantly answered. "Yep."

"Nice. Did you get to meet her?"

"Yep."

"You're a man of many words, brother."

Liam folded his arms and leaned on the counter. "Guess I just don't kiss and tell."

Max froze mid-swipe, his brows lifting and a sly grin tugging at his mouth. "You dog! No way!"

Liam just grinned back, returning momentarily to the happiness he'd felt in L.A.

"How the hell did that happen?"

He shrugged. "We met in the hotel bar. I bought her a drink."

"And?"

Liam ran one palm over his tired neck. "And what? You want a blow-by-blow?"

"Hell, yeah!"

"Sorry, not gonna happen, Max."

"You gotta give me something! Did you two make a connection?"

Liam stared at the tile floor, not really seeing it. "Off the fucking charts."

"I'm happy for you, man. You seeing her again?"

Liam shook his head. The same pain he'd felt waking up that morning and finding her gone flashed through him.

"What? Why not? You got her number, didn't you?"

"She snuck out the next morning."

Max frowned. "That sucks. Any idea why?"

"No clue. Everything was great… at least I thought

it was."

"Sorry, man." Max was quiet for a moment and then continued, trying to inject a lightness to his words. "Chicks. Sometimes there's just no figurin' 'em out."

Liam nodded. "Guess so."

"She know where you work?"

"We talked about the show." He frowned. "I think I mentioned the shop."

"Well, maybe she'll call here."

Liam rocked forward and stood. "Yeah, maybe. Let's go get a beer."

"Sounds like a plan. Did you lock the front door?"

Liam headed to do the task.

"You know we could always drive out to the farm to have a beer."

"Malee's not gonna mind?"

"Just because I got married didn't mean you had to move out. It's your home just as much as it is mine, Rory's and Jameson's."

"I just thought with Jameson moved into his new place with Ava and the baby, maybe it was time I left, too, and gave you some privacy."

"Liam, I never asked you to go."

"I know, but you've got Ben now, and Mrs. Larsen's living there, helping take care of him, and look that's all great, but I just feel like the third wheel, you know? And now with Malee pregnant—"

"Are you happy living in town?"

Liam shrugged. "Yeah, sure. Why?"

"You'd rather live in that tiny apartment over the bakery?"

"Hey, livin' over the bakery has its advantages; breakfast is only steps away and the place always smells like fresh baked bread. Can't beat that, man."

Max chuckled. "Yeah, as long as you don't put on twenty pounds."

Liam patted his flat stomach. "That's what sit-ups are for. That and I've been running a lot."

"Hmm. Yeah, I heard you've been running. You should stop by the gym and spend some time with the punching bag. Or I could always go a couple rounds in the ring with you."

"I'm not suicidal. Thanks."

Max put Liam in a headlock and pretended to punch him in the face. "You sure? Maybe I could rearrange this mug for you."

CHAPTER FIVE

Velvet took a walk through town one afternoon. She had to get out of the shop and away from Vano. He was a shit artist, and she knew he was using her as a draw for business, but she felt like she was useless.

Being back in Grand Junction was bittersweet. She hated working for Vano, but Liam was here. She drifted aimlessly toward Main Street, turning right and heading down the block. Maybe she'd stop and get a Frappe. Her steps slowed as she approached one storefront window with colorfully painted silk garments and artwork all beautifully arranged. While she appreciated them, she couldn't help the pull that turned her head to look to the shop across the street.

Brothers Ink. *His* shop. Liam O'Rourke.

Velvet remembered him. How could she forget?

She had decided to work for her brother, even though it put her back in her family's clutches, because she'd be near Liam. Try as she may, now that she'd seen him in LA, she couldn't stay away. She had become obsessed. She'd walked by the place at least once a week since she'd come back.

Liam had made her want more—to remember how she was before she'd become so jaded.

She stared at the storefront window, longing for the missed opportunity and what she could never have. They'd spent one incredible night together in LA. The sex had been great, but that wasn't the first time his hands had run over her skin. She remembered the first time he'd put his hands on her and how sweet he'd seemed, and then later how devastated he'd been.

Everything about that day was burned into her brain—the good and the bad…

The bell above the door tinkled as Velvet entered the shop—the one her mother and brother had picked out. They had said it was ripe for the picking. It was a new shop, just getting started in the business and therefore its reputation was on shaky ground. Her mother said they would pay dearly to protect that fledgling reputation, making them the perfect mark.

Velvet's eyes strayed nervously to the art on the wall. Photos of tattoos they had done and drawings of art they could do stretched from the plate glass window to the counter. Their work was good—better than most shops her mother and brother sent her to.

Boots scuffed across the wooden floor, and she turned. Her mouth parted at the man who moved behind the reception counter.

He was tall, muscular, and gruff looking, with brows that slashed deep over brown eyes. Ink ran up both arms, disappearing into the flannel shirt he wore with the sleeves cut off.

Peeking out from the open plackets of his shirt were words scrawled in ink across his collarbone. *I can't change the past and I can't predict the future.*

Wasn't that the truth?

"Can I help you?" he asked in a voice so low it rumbled. The question drew her eyes from his skin.

"I want a tattoo, but I don't have an appointment."

His eyes roved over her body slowly before returning to her face. "You gotta be eighteen to get ink, sweetheart."

"I am," she lied.

His brow lifted. "You got some ID?"

She reached in her bag and took out her wallet.

Taking out the fake ID, she passed it to the man.

His gaze shifted from it to her. Apparently satisfied, he held it out. "You know what you want?"

She nodded.

He glanced at the clock. "I've got some time before my next appointment. If it's not too involved, I could probably knock it out."

She pulled a piece of folded paper from her pocket. It wasn't what her mother told her to get, but she didn't care. This one time she was getting what she wanted.

She handed it across the counter to him.

His eyes met hers as he took it. He glanced down and nodded. "Okay. Shouldn't be a problem." He grabbed a clipboard from under the counter and slid it toward her. There was a release form clipped to it. He held out a pen and pointed to several areas. "Read this and initial each section, then sign the bottom."

She did as he asked, feeling his eyes on her the whole time. She pretended to read each section and scribbled her initials and then her name at the bottom. When she held it out to him, their eyes met, and she felt some emotion zing through her. It affected her so much that she dropped her gaze and sucked her lips into her mouth.

The clipboard slipped from her hand as he took it,

and she glanced up. Just a quick dart of her eyes, but she caught the motion as he jerked his head. "Come on back to my station."

Following him around the corner, she took in the two stations on each side of the narrow shop. He stopped at the first one on the left and patted his hand on the bottom of the adjustable chair. "Have a seat, sweetheart."

As she did, he studied the scrap of paper. It was a hand drawn sketch of a bunch of wildflowers and a butterfly.

"Where did you want this?"

She lifted her arm and pointed at the tender flesh on the inside of her bicep.

"Okay. Did you want it with some color?"

She bit her lip indecisively. "Umm...."

He cocked his head. "You mind if I suggest something to you?"

"No."

"Let me sketch something out." He turned to the low counter under a mirror on the wall and began drawing, his big hand moving with quick, strong sweeps. Everything about the way he mastered the pen in his hand indicated he was a man confident in his abilities. She began to relax. A few moments later he twisted back and turned the paper to face her. "How about this?"

It was like the design she'd given him but a hundred times better. She smiled. "Yes. Do that. I love it."

"You want color?"

She shook her head.

"It's a simple design. I can draw it freehand, unless you want me to take the time to do up a transfer."

She met his warm brown eyes. His appearance was intimidating, but the look in his eyes was soft, almost tender.

"You'll do a good job? You won't mess it up? This tattoo…it's important to me."

"I won't mess it up."

"You promise?"

He made an X over his heart. "Cross my heart."

She found that endearing, as was his smile, and she knew she could trust him to do this tattoo with all the care as if it were a major piece that cost hundreds of dollars. "Okay."

"How big do you want it?"

She gestured toward the paper. "That size."

He held it against her skin. "Like this?"

She glanced down and shook her head. "I want it

running vertically."

He turned the paper. "This way?"

"Yes, right there."

He pulled it away, and as he snapped on some gloves, his eyes met hers. "This your first tattoo, sweetheart?"

"Yes," she murmured the lie, knowing her other tattoos were well covered.

He cleaned the area and then held the paper back up. "Here, right?"

She nodded, and he made a couple of marks on her skin to make sure he got it exactly where she wanted it, then set the paper on his work tray.

"How's your pain threshold?"

"I'll be fine."

"Then why do you look so nervous?" When she didn't reply, he patted her knee. "Don't worry. This shouldn't be too bad."

When he was finished and had cleaned the area, he held a mirror up for her to see the ink marked into her skin.

He hadn't lied. The tattoo hadn't been bad at all. He'd treated her gently, joking with her and keeping her talking to distract from the discomfort. As she'd watched him work, she'd soon realized she was in skilled hands.

She couldn't help the small smile that pulled at her mouth as she examined his work.

"Are you happy with it?"

She looked up to see his eyes on her and could tell he was sincere in his question. He truly wanted her to be pleased with the work he'd done. "Yes. It's perfect. I love it."

"Good, darlin'. Glad to hear it." He gave her a cocky grin, took the mirror from her, and quickly salved and bandaged her arm. When he was through, he pulled his gloves off with a snap, tossed them in the trash, and held his hand out to help her down.

She slipped her hand into his warm palm. He'd touched her plenty in the process of tattooing her, but there was something intimate about holding a man's hand. The feel of hers in his much larger one, the way his closed around her fingers, how he lingered a bit longer than necessary before almost reluctantly dropping away as he gazed down at her from his towering height.

He settled his palm on the small of her back as he guided her back to the front, making her feel protected, as crazy as that sounded.

Unbidden, the thought floated through her mind of

what it would be like to have a man like him someday.

Now that the work was done, the high from getting the tattoo was beginning to wear off and the fear of what was to come when her mother saw it took hold. And even worse… the humiliation she would endure when her mother dragged her back in here and pretended to be outraged that this shop had "put a hideous tattoo" on her underaged daughter.

It was a scam her mother had used over and over since the time Velvet had come home with her first ink. Her mother had dragged her to the shop and berated the owner, threatening to sue him for every penny he had. After all, everyone knew gypsy girls didn't get tattoos, and especially not of English boy's names. It was an affront that had infuriated her mother. That is, until the man had offered her five hundred dollars to sign the consent form and go away. Her mother had signed and left with the cash in hand, but she'd done so with a new plan in mind, a new way for the family to make money. A *new con*, and it was one that would make them thousands.

Suddenly her daughter's marketability on the

marriage front took a backseat to her greed. She no longer cared that her daughter's skin would be tattooed, as long as there was a payoff in it for her.

Velvet nodded politely as Liam went over after care instructions with her and handed her a printout with it all spelled out. She'd heard them enough times in the last few months.

She paid and glanced at him one last time as he stood there with his hands on the counter, his gorgeous arms on display and a smile on his face.

She took a moment to take in that warm expression, because she wouldn't see it again when she returned later, her mother hauling her in by her arm to play out their con.

As Velvet stood on the sidewalk and stared at the shop across the street, she knew how special that memory was to her, every moment crystal clear.

Velvet had had a secret crush on Liam ever since, and she'd felt incredibly guilty over what happened.

Over the years, she had all the other tattoos covered with better, beautiful ink, trying to erase the reminders from her skin, but try as she might, and as stunning as her new ink was, she could never erase the guilt and shame she still carried. She'd covered every tattoo; that is, all but one—all but his. She could never bring herself to have Liam's covered over. He'd been the only one to show her any care. And even when her mother's scam was apparent, Liam had seen the shame on Velvet's face. He'd recognized that her mother was using her.

She'd had tears in her eyes when she'd whispered, "I'm sorry."

He wanted to have her mother brought up on charges, but his brother, Jameson, apparently knew what kind of people he was dealing with. "It'd be a waste of time, Liam. They'll be gone by morning."

CHAPTER SIX

A week later –

"Brothers Ink," Liam answered the phone. The rumble of a Harley pulling up at the curb drew his gaze toward the storefront window. A man and young girl climbed off the bike. He immediately recognized the man. Ryder, the President of a local MC had been getting all his ink from Jameson for years. Liam didn't recognize the girl, but she looked like she couldn't be more than sixteen.

The voice on the other end of the line drew his attention back. "Yes, ma'am. We're open until nine. I've got that product in stock if you want to stop by and pick it up tonight. Yes, ma'am. Thank you."

The bell over the door tinkled and the two strode inside. It was obvious before Ryder reached the counter that he was pissed.

"Can I help you?" Liam asked, hanging the phone up.

Ryder glared at the girl with him. "Show him."

The teen rolled her eyes, but held out her arm. Liam took in the red angry tattoo that wasn't healing well.

"Can you fix it?" Ryder growled.

Liam took the girl's wrist gently in his hand and dipped his head to study the tattoo, turning her arm to see the full ink. Two Koi fish entwined scrolled around her arm. Not only was it not healing well, the shading was horrid, and the line-work was complete shit. He whistled softly, his eyes lifting to meet hers. "Let me guess. House of Ink?"

She frowned, her bewildered expression moving to her father, then back to Liam. "H-how did you know?"

"Around here we call it House of *Crap*. We get about three or four of their customers a week wanting us to fix their shit work. Had two girls in here yesterday with some really bad ink; one of theirs was badly infected."

The biker huffed out a breath and shoved away from the counter. "Christ, Molly! You wanted ink, you shoulda told me. I would've brought you here in the first place."

"I'm sorry, Dad. I didn't know. Ronnie said they were cool and—"

Her father finished the sentence for her. "And

they'd tattoo you even though you were underage."

She nodded.

"I woulda signed the consent and gotten Jameson to do the work."

"Mom said you wouldn't let me."

"You're mom doesn't know everything, Mol. You want something, you come to me and we talk about it. Maybe you get it, maybe you don't."

"Okay, sorry."

He looked at Liam. "Can you fix it?"

"Yeah, I'm sure we can once the infection heals."

"Infection? Goddamn it!" Ryder growled and glared at Molly. "I shoulda busted that guy in the mouth."

Liam frowned. "What guy?"

"I took her down there to show 'em what shit they did to my baby-girl, but the guy who did the work wasn't around. Just some smart-mouthed guy at one of the chairs and—"

"Dad!"

Liam nodded, completely understanding this guy's rage. "Yeah, I'd love nothing more than to see them shut down. I hate to say that about another shop, but they've got no business being in this industry. They're the kind that give the profession a bad name."

Ryder huffed. "Yeah, they do. Anyway, the chick working there apologized. It threw me for a minute because I recognized her from the magazines. Thought it was weird someone like her was there."

"They've got a chick working down there now?"

"Yeah. You know the famous one in all the pictures?"

Liam frowned, not sure he did.

"Shit. What's her name?" He snapped his fingers a couple of times. "Fuck, I can't remember—Wait, it was her. The one in that picture." He pointed toward Liam's workstation.

Liam twisted to look over his shoulder, his eyes landing on the calendar. No way. It couldn't be. "Velvet?"

"Yeah, Velvet. That's her name."

Liam's brows shot up. "You're saying Velvet Jones is down at House of Crap Ink? What the hell would she be doing down at that shithole?"

Ryder shrugged. "Fuck if I know. But I'm tellin' you, it was her, sure as shit. Nice chick, too. Apologized profusely about the work that asshole did on Molly.

Gave all the money back plus a hundred bucks."

Liam barely heard what the man said. All he could think about was that Velvet—*his* Velvet—was here in Grand Junction. Hell, she was just a couple of blocks away. His eyes strayed to the window.

"So what about fixing Molly's tattoo?"

Liam mumbled, "Yeah, I'll put her down for a session at the end of the month. But you should have a doctor look at her arm. The infection needs to be treated."

"Yeah, more money this is gonna cost me," the biker grumbled. "Thanks, man. Come on, Mol."

Liam stood, his palms on the counter, one thumb tapping rapidly as his mind reeled.

The tinkling of the bell over the door as Ryder and his daughter left broke him from his trance, and he twisted to look over his shoulder. "Hey, Max, I need to step out for a couple minutes. You good?"

The buzzing of the tattoo machine paused as Max glanced up from the customer he was working on. "Everything okay?"

Liam straightened. "Yeah, man. I've just got something important I need to check on."

"All right. But be quick. You've got that guy comin' in to finish that dragon at four."

Liam glanced at the clock. It gave him forty minutes. "I'll be back."

CHAPTER SEVEN

Liam walked into House of Ink, and his eyes traveled around the shop, taking in the grungy floors, the lack of sketches on the wall, and no trace of disinfectant.

All the warning signs and red flags that should scream to a customer to turn around and walk out were there: dirt, gross smells, the needles they'd probably reused. An artist—and he used the term loosely—was talking with a client. The man was making some excuse to avoid showing the kid his portfolios. Liam's eyes hit the price list on the wall. They offered crazy cheap tattoos. The place, if it were cleaned regularly should smell like disinfectant. Instead it smelled like unwashed bodies.

He knew practices varied based on the studio, but ultimately it should be evident that needles are being sterilized or are single-use. The artists should always open the tools and tubes in front of the client before putting needle to skin.

As Liam watched for a while, that was not the case here.

The guy at the counter continued to rush the client toward a design and push him into getting the tattoo. In the business it was called tattoo bullying.

House of Ink was the definition of everything bad in the tattoo world. While Brothers Ink was everything that bespoke of the art of tattooing—it was clean, organized, and with a sleek and contemporary interior, and artists who were extremely talented, with work so far above the slipshod crap the men working here put out.

Liam observed one of the artists, a young punk of a kid who couldn't be old enough to have much experience, begin to clean a young girl's skin without first putting on gloves. When he reached for his tattoo machine, still without gloves and, from the looks of it, without changing the needle for a new one, Liam had to intervene. There was no way he was going to stand by and let that girl be infected with a dirty needle in unsterilized conditions right in front of his eyes.

"Hey, man, you change that needle out?"

The kid paused and looked over at him. "You talkin' to me?"

"Yeah, I'm talkin' to you."

"Ain't none of your business."

"Where are your gloves?"

He paused again. "What is your problem, man? You don't work here. I'm the tattoo artist, and I know what I'm doing."

The girl in his chair suddenly looked concerned. "Wait. He's right. You're supposed to be wearing gloves, aren't you?"

He patted her shoulder. "Don't you worry about it. I know what I'm doing."

"Apparently not, buddy. Or you'd have changed out that needle for a sterile one or a single use one, and you'd have gloves on. Did you even clean the tattoo area?"

"Look, mister, you need to get the fuck outta here. I don't need you tellin' me shit or scaring my customers."

"Sweetheart," Liam looked at the girl, "I'm just lookin' out for you. I work down at Brothers Ink, and I know what I'm talking about. I'm just trying to save you from a bad infection."

The artist tossed his tattoo machine down on his workstation and stood, charging toward Liam. He pointed toward the door. "I done told you to get the fuck outta here, you son-of-a-bitch!"

Liam stood his ground. "Where's the owner? 'Cause it sure as shit ain't you."

"He ain't here. Now get the fuck out!"

"You want to try and make me, pipsqueak?"

The skinny kid shoved Liam, but Liam barely moved an inch.

"Stop it! Please, stop!"

From the corner of his eye, Liam saw two people come out of the back. He felt an arm on his, and he swiveled his head at the sound of the feminine voice he knew right away. He'd been expecting to find her here, but still, her sudden appearance had him freezing in motion, his words deserting him. All he could do was stare at her.

"Please leave." She would barely meet his eyes.

"You want me to leave, then come outside and talk to me."

The man who had followed her out of the back spoke. "She's not going anywhere with you."

"Shut up, Vano," Velvet snapped at the man, and Liam couldn't help noticing the tick in the man's jaw when she spoke to him that way. She looked like she'd even surprised herself with those words. Liam wondered who this guy was, but the tension in the shop had their emotions charged, and for some reason

Vano let it slide. She jerked her gaze back to Liam. "Fine. Come on."

Liam trailed behind her out the door. The shop sat on the corner, and so she led him around the wall and out of sight of the storefront window.

CHAPTER EIGHT

Liam followed Velvet out the door and around the corner, irritation rolling through him. He ran a hand through his hair, pacing away, and then spinning back to her. In three steps he had her up against the wall. Wide eyes stared up at him. He only held them a moment before his gaze dropped to her lips, and then he was a goner. Christ, he couldn't help himself.

His mouth descended on hers, capturing her soft lips under his. He felt and heard her quick intake of breath through her nose, and knew he'd taken her by surprise, but he didn't give a damn.

She recovered quickly, and her palms settled on his chest, but they didn't push him away. After a moment her mouth softened and opened for him. He took the invitation, and his tongue swept inside. Her head fell back, and her hands slid up to twine around his neck. He crowded her against the wall until her soft breasts pressed against the unrelenting muscle of his chest. Damn, that felt good, but he was a selfish bastard, and he wanted more. His hands landed on her hips, then smoothed up under her soft tank top to the warm skin of her curves, settling at her tiny waist. His grip tightened, and he dragged her pelvis against his, letting her feel the erection that pushed against the placket of his jeans, yearning toward her. He rubbed against her until she was moaning under his mouth, and her hands clutched him tighter to her.

When he finally broke the kiss to breathe, they stared speechless at each other. The need in him welled up, and he fought to tamp it back down.

Recovering first, she glanced toward the door. "Umm…you need to go."

Was she worried one of those assholes would come outside? He wasn't. They were the last things on his mind right now. "Why'd you run out on me?"

Her brows arched. "I didn't run out on you. I merely got dressed and left that morning."

"Why didn't you at least say goodbye? We had a connection. We both felt it. We *still* feel it. So don't pretend that night was nothing to you."

She swallowed but didn't deny it, and Liam was grateful for that at least, but he needed more. He lifted his chin to the shop. "What time do you get out of here tonight?"

Cute little frown lines formed as her brows drew together. "Why?"

He couldn't resist pressing his mouth softly to them, touching the spot just between her brows. When he pulled back, her face softened. Had no one ever shown her tenderness? "You're going to meet me tonight."

She pushed him back a few inches, shaking her head. "No I'm not. I can't. I—"

"Yes, you can and you are. And we're gonna talk this out." He glanced to the side. "Not here on the street, but at my place where we've got some privacy."

"Liam—"

"I live in the apartment above Heinzelmann's Bakery, down the street from Brothers Ink. It's the blue door next to the bakery entrance. Can't miss it. My apartment is top of the stairs."

"I-I don't know, I—"

"You don't show, I'll turn up here again tomorrow and every day until you do. That the way you want to play this?" He wasn't about to let her off the hook.

Her defiant little chin came up, and all he could

think about was kissing that mouth again. "Don't boss me around. I don't like it."

He grinned. "You'll get used to it."

"Used to it?" There was a snap in her voice.

He bumped his nose to hers. "Yeah, I can be bossy, I admit it. But I can also be sweet and attentive and devoted."

"Devoted?"

"Loving and affectionate and devoted to your every need."

"My every need?" Her brow arched with her smirk.

He pulled her lower half against him for another slow rub. "Every single one."

"That's quite a promise."

"One I intend to keep. Tonight." He sealed the promise with a kiss and let her go, leaving her standing open-mouthed. He smiled to himself as he walked back toward Brothers Ink, a new jaunt in his step. He smiled at passersby; the sun seemed brighter, hell, the whole day seemed brighter. Yes, things were definitely looking up.

CHAPTER NINE

Velvet hesitated, her knuckles inches from Liam's door. Her heart wanted her to go in, but her head told her this was a bad idea—for so many reasons—first and foremost because she hadn't been honest with Liam. What was she doing? She knew if she let herself get close to him, she wouldn't be able to resist. And then where would she be? She'd fall for him, and it would be hard and fast, and when she hit bottom and he found out her secrets, what then? He'd hate her. He'd want nothing more to do with her. Would she be able to handle that? Would being with him now be worth the pain that was sure to follow?

He'd been the mark in one of her family's cons for God's sake. She knew better than to get involved with him. That was rule number one.

She listed all the reasons being here, standing poised with her hand an inch from his door was a terrible idea. None of that mattered to her heart, though. And in the war between her head and her heart, it was no contest. It never had been and never would be, not where Liam was concerned. She took a deep breath and rapped against the wood.

When Liam opened the door, his eyes swept over her, taking in every inch. As his gaze traveled the length of her body, a tingling flush moved over her skin, almost as if he were already touching her.

He stood before her in a tight t-shirt, his jeans hanging low on his hips.

Being here, seeing him again and knowing what might happen here tonight—hell, what probably *would* happen here tonight if she were being completely honest with herself—had her pulse beating rapidly and her breathing accelerating. Then seeing him—all that was him—took the words from her, and she had to lick her lips. "Hello."

She barely got the word out before he drew her flush against him and claimed her mouth for a kiss. It was hot and passionate, and the way he took what he wanted was totally alpha male, and she loved everything about it, but she knew she had to keep her wits about her if she was going to maneuver this "reunion" with care.

She pushed away, breaking the kiss. "I thought you wanted to talk."

He pulled her back. "We'll get to that."

After a longer, deeper kiss, he lifted her up and carried her down the hall to his bedroom.

Velvet had just barely time to take in a few quick impressions of his place. It was small with a living room that faced the front street on the left, a dining room/kitchen combination on the right, and a hallway in the middle that led to a bedroom. She noticed a flat screen TV and shelving cubes stacked under the windows filled with what might have been record albums. A brown leather couch and rustic wooden coffee table flashed by as he carried her down the hall.

The next thing she knew, her back was to the mattress of a big bed, and he came down on top of her. His weight settled over her, one leg thrown across hers, his upper body supported by his elbows, giving her enough room to breath.

His mouth ate at hers, nipping and licking, his tongue sweeping inside again and again until she was lifting her head to follow his, wanting more every time he retreated.

It was a mating dance as old as time. Her hands slid over his broad shoulders to twine around his neck, pulling him down for more.

His body moved against hers, and she felt the proof of his desire. It rubbed against her thigh, long and hard. Suddenly it was as if no time at all had passed since last they'd been together in his LA hotel room.

He lifted his head and one hand brushed the hair from her face, his eyes tracking the movement of his palm. "I love your hair. It's so soft and silky." He threaded his fingers through it, then grabbed a handful, tipping her head back for his kiss.

She loved the control he took and willingly gave it over to him.

His mouth trailed down her neck, his lips pressing soft kisses along her skin.

She exposed her neck further to give him better access. His warm mouth closed over a vulnerable spot and sucked deep, and her eyes fluttered closed as she reveled in the sensation. She knew there'd be a mark there tomorrow, but she didn't care. She wanted his mark.

A big warm palm closed over her breast and squeezed, and a low moan rumbled up from her throat. His fingers went to the buttons of her shirt, making quick work of them. A second later he'd tugged the cups of her bra down, and her breasts popped free.

"Beautiful," he murmured, and when he did

nothing more, she tipped her head down, her eyes opening. He was motionless, his gaze locked on her chest. Then slowly, his hand moved over her skin, his thumb brushing softly over her nipple. Once, twice, three times.

Velvet's breath came in soft pants as her nipples tightened into buds of tightly bundled nerve endings. The anticipation of his mouth on them was sweet torture.

Finally, he leaned down, and the flat of his tongue swiped over one red bud. Then he blew, and the sensation had her writhing and thrusting her chest up for more.

"Your nipples are just as responsive as I remember."

Their eyes met as images of the night they'd spent together flashed between them.

He grinned and lowered his head, giving her what she longed for. His mouth closed over her nipple and tugged deep and long.

Her back arched, thrusting her breast up even farther, and her hands clawed at his sides, wanting the sensation to go on forever.

A jolt of erotic response shot straight to her pussy, and she knew she was drenched for him.

As if he read her mind, his hand moved down her body and his palm cupped her inner thigh, spreading her wide. He slid his thick fingers to the juncture of her thighs where he kneaded and rubbed and teased. All the while, his mouth sucked and licked and nipped, first one nipple, then the other until she was a puddle of need writhing under him.

Suddenly he raised off her and stood at the foot of the bed. He grabbed her knees and yanked her forward until her legs dangled off the mattress. He worked at the fastenings of her jeans and tugged them off her.

She shrugged her blouse off her shoulders and pulled her bra free.

She lay there in just her panties while he tore his shirt over his head.

God, she'd forgotten how gorgeous his bare chest was. She barely had time to take it in before he bent, shoving down his pants and dropping to his knees between her legs.

His hands stroked slowly up her thighs, his gaze on her panty-covered pussy.

She lifted her hand to him, wanting him to come up the bed and fuck her. "Please, baby. I need you."

He shook his head. "I've waited too long for this, angel. I've lain awake too many nights remembering the taste of you on my tongue to rush this now." His eyes bore into hers. "You gonna let me take my time?"

She nodded, eager to please him. Her response came out soft and needy. "Yes, baby."

"Good girl."

His fingers curled around the scrap of lace that was all that hid her from his eyes, and he dragged them down her legs.

When she was bare to him, he pressed her thighs wider, making room for those broad shoulders of his as he moved closer. His thumbs brushed over her pussy, and her hips shot off the bed in response.

He dipped and kissed his way up her thighs, her eyes slid closed, and she drowned in the sensations of his beard and tongue tickling their way up her leg. With every soft press of his lips, with every lap of his tongue, she fell a little more for him.

He had a way of teasing and tormenting her body until she'd do anything… give anything to have the release he held just out of reach. God, she couldn't trust her body, the way it responded to him. He had more control over it than she did.

He paused, his mouth hovering just over her pussy. She trembled, trying not to move an inch, not even daring to breathe.

His hand came up, and he lightly traced her pussy with his thumb. "I've waited a long time to taste you again, Velvet. Dreamed about it night after night."

Her body vibrated until every nerve ending was alive with anticipation.

"Are you going to tease me all night?"

"If you want me to, I will. For hours, baby; just say the word." His thumbs played until wetness flooded down. He dipped his head and lapped at her, then lifted with a groan. "Goddamn, I've never tasted anything so fucking good."

"I need you so bad."

"Just relax, baby girl. We've got all night."

What seemed like hours later, her pussy was swollen from his attention and her thighs were tingling from his beard. She was a melted pile of mush, unable to move, her skin slick with sweat and her chest heaving. God, she had no idea orgasms could be like that. No other man had ever been able to draw one after another from her body like Liam did.

"Please, Liam, no more," she panted.

He slid up the bed, his weight settling on top of her

at long last.

He brushed the hair from her forehead and dipped down to kiss her lips. Pulling back, his eyes locked with hers. "You ready for me, beautiful?"

Her breathing was still coming fast, but she smiled up at him. "So wet, so ready."

His eyes darkened at her words, and his hips lifted. A moment later he thrust inside her. When he was fully seated, he stilled. "My dick's been hard for you since you walked in the door. Been taking my time, making this so good for you, but this, babe? *This* is where I've wanted to be again since the morning you walked out that hotel room door."

Before she could formulate a reply—not that it was easy to form words with all the sensations zinging through her body—his mouth closed over hers, and he began to move, drawing slowly out and thrusting in just as slowly, dragging along every nerve ending, drawing out the sensations as artfully as she remembered. The man was good at this, superb, a damn master at it. He stroked her skin with one hand, moving over her chest and hips while his other cradled her head. He pressed kisses along her temple, her cheekbone, her jaw, and down her neck to eventually climb her breast to her nipple.

Gradually his pace picked up, and his head dipped, his eyes focusing on where their bodies were joined. As he watched, his movements became more urgent. Soon his skin was slick with sweat as his strokes went on and on.

Big hands slipped under her, palms closing over her ass cheeks and tilting her hips up. The new angle had each long stroke rubbing over that very sensitive bundle of nerves inside her while he reached around and brushed his thumb back and forth across her clit.

The combination had her gasping and panting as she chugged closer to the top of the roller coaster that would soon bring her to the precipice and over the edge.

"Oh, yes. *Yes,*" she moaned. "Right there. Don't stop."

"I won't, Velvet."

His body slammed into her, again and again, dragging across all those nerves, and the whole while that big calloused thumb of his kept at her clit in slow tight circles until she couldn't hold back any longer.

"Come for me, sweet Velvet."

At his soft command, her back arched and she felt

her body explode.

As she floated down from ten thousand feet in a long gentle free fall, he shifted, hands grasping her hips. He pounded into her until he too climaxed with a roar.

When his body collapsed down on top of her, she wrapped her arms around him, stroking his back as he breathed heavily from the exertion.

After a few moments of her tender caresses, he pressed soft kisses along her collarbone. His arms tightened, and he rolled until he was on his back and she was tight to his side, his arms wrapped around her.

She skated her fingers over his chest, tracing the colorful lines of his tattoos until his hand came up and closed over hers, stilling her movements and bringing her knuckles to his mouth for a kiss.

"That was so good," she whispered.

"That was better than good, angel. Best I've ever had."

"Me, too."

She smiled against his skin, and when he tipped his head, she knew he'd felt it. She tilted hers up to see that fact confirmed by the happy grin on his face.

"Don't go getting all smug on me," she teased.

His hand flattened on his chest. "Me? Smug? Not a chance. I'm just over here bein' all grateful and shit."

"Grateful, huh? Not exactly the emotion I was going for."

"How about devotion, adoration, worship?"

She slapped his taut stomach lightly. "Quit teasing."

He jumped as her palm connected and chuckled, then rolled her to her back again. "You want teasing, I'm all too happy to oblige, lady, if you think you can take more."

"No, no. No more. I'm worn out." She giggled.

He smiled down at her, his fingers lightly rubbing her forehead until her eyes slid closed. "You look happy."

She indulged in the feeling of his fingertips trailing over her skin a moment longer. "I am."

"Good. I plan to keep you that way."

She opened her eyes and met his gaze. "Do you, now?"

"If you let me."

She searched his face. It would be so easy to let him.

When she didn't reply, he prodded, "We gonna do

this?"

Her teeth nibbled on her bottom lip, and his eyes dropped to the motion. "I don't know, Liam."

Her response had his eyes flicking up to hers. "What don't you know?"

Needing an excuse, she glanced away and lied. "I've been hurt before."

"I'm not looking to hurt you, Velvet. Far from it. I just think we have something here, and we owe it to ourselves to see where it goes."

Her eyes shifted to his hypnotic gaze, and she got lost in the depths of the warm brown orbs. God, he could talk her into anything if she let him, and in this moment, she wanted to let him.

When she stayed quiet, he finally asked, "You don't feel the same?"

She couldn't bear the look of doubt that flashed across his face. "I do."

He brushed the back of his fingers down her cheek. "I'm not gonna let you run again."

She couldn't help but wonder if he'd come to regret those words. "I don't want to run." And in that she was completely honest. Running from him was the last thing she wanted to do.

He grinned, and she loved to see happiness on

his face and to know she'd put it there. "Good, because you're spending the night."

"You going all alpha again, bossing me around?" She pretended to object, but deep in her heart she loved him taking control.

"Gonna try, but somehow I've got the feelin' you're the one who's gonna end up with all the power in this relationship."

She traced her finger along the groove made by his grin and returned his smile, truly happy for the first time in a long time.

CHAPTER TEN

Velvet strolled hand-in-hand with Liam out of the bakery that occupied the storefront under his apartment, stepping out into the bright morning sun and sipping a to-go cup of hot coffee. She met his eyes over the rim, thoughts of last night dancing in her head. He winked at her as if he'd read her mind. It felt good. It felt warm and wonderful, and it filled her with joy—the kind she hadn't ever known. He brought her hand to his mouth and kissed the tips of her fingers then tucked her up against his side as they moved down the street.

"Know what I was thinking?" his deep voice rumbled softly in her ear as he dipped low, his beard tickling her cheek.

She tilted her face up to his, not hiding the joy that she was sure sparkled in her eyes. "What's that?"

"That I could get used to this."

"Used to what?"

"Sharing coffee and walking you to work every morning."

She let out a soft giggle. "Oh, could you, now?"

"Yes, ma'am. Sure could."

"Hmm. I could get used to it, too. And those fried doughnut things we just had were amazing."

"Yep. Can't forget Mrs. Heinzelmann's Spritzkuchen. Makes the best in town."

"I've never had them before."

"Girl, you've been missing out."

Her eyes moved over his happy face. It wasn't the doughnuts she was thinking of when she answered, "I do believe I have."

"I mean to change all that, Velvet, if you let me." Something in the way he said those words and the suddenly serious expression on his face had her believing him. This man could change so many things for her if she would just let herself be open enough to trust in what they had.

When she didn't answer right away, he turned to face her, backing her to the wall. His solemn eyes pinned hers. "You gonna let me?"

Staring up at him, she could do nothing but acquiesce. No words of denial would come from her mouth. "Yes, Liam. I'll let you."

"Good. Glad we got that settled." A broad grin spread across his face, and it absolutely lit up his whole expression. He dipped his head and touched his lips softly to hers, then stepped back and tugged on their linked hands. "Come on, pretty girl."

By the time Velvet had finished the last of her coffee, they had arrived at House of Ink. They paused outside. Liam's expression darkened as he looked up at the signage and briefly at the plate glass window.

She tried to release his hand but he tugged her a step closer, refusing to let her go just yet. He captured her eyes, bringing his face inches from hers.

"You're off tomorrow, right? The shop's not open on Sunday, is it?"

"No, it's not open."

"So, you're off then?"

"Yes."

"Good. I'm taking you somewhere."

She couldn't hide the happiness from her face. "Oh, really. Where?"

"It's a surprise."

"What time are you picking me up?"

"Well, since you'll be wakin' up in my bed, I guess we won't have to worry about that."

"Well, aren't you the presumptuous one?"

"Makin' up for all that wasted lost time, which, by the way, was totally your fault."

"Haven't I made up for it by moving to your town?"

He gave her palm a kiss. "It's a good start. I'll come up with some other things you can do to make it up to me."

She grinned and looked behind her. "I really should go inside."

He glanced at the hours on the door. "See you at nine."

"Ten," she corrected. Then laughed at the pout on his face. "I have to go home and get a change of clothes at least. Anything I need to bring for this adventure tomorrow?"

"A jacket and sunglasses."

"Hmm, a small hint. So we'll be outside, I take it?"

"The lady is quick."

"Don't you forget it."

"No chance of that." He caught her face in his hands and tugged her flush against him, dipping his head for a kiss. It was longer than the last one but shorter than either of them would have liked. He broke off and kissed the tip of her nose. "See you tonight, Velvet."

"Goodbye, Liam."

She turned and let herself into the store then relocked it. Liam waited until she was safely inside before he turned and walked away with a final wave.

She returned his wave with a smile, then walked to the rear of the shop and set her purse down at the small cubicle Vano had set up for her. She was touching up her lipstick when she heard Vano come in the back door. She turned.

"Hey."

He glanced over at her. "Good, you're here. Come with me. I've got a deposit I want you to take to the bank. First Federal two blocks down on Third Avenue. Know where that is?"

She nodded and followed him into his office. He knelt by the safe and twirled the tumbler. A moment later he had it open, and her eyes widened when they fell on the stacks of cash inside.

He grabbed some, counted out an amount, shoved it in a zippered deposit bag, and locked the safe.

"Why do you have so much money in the safe, Vano?"

His stern eyes pinned her. "I've just let it build up, is all. Haven't taken a deposit in a while. I think it's time you take over that job. I hate doing it. It's a pain in the ass."

She supposed his explanation made sense. Still, it seemed like an awful lot of money.

When he rose to his feet, he bent over the desk and filled out the deposit form. "It's $9875.00 Just below the daily limit of ten thousand."

"Why does that matter?"

"Anything over that has to be reported."

"Reported? To who?"

"The Feds. Homeland security shit. We can thank terrorism for that bullshit."

"Oh."

"I've written it out. You just take it to the counter and get a receipt. They ask any questions, just shrug and play the dumb employee. Got it?"

"What would they ask?"

"Hell if I know. Sometimes bankers are noisy. Get all in your business. Fucking bullshit is what it is. Reason I don't want to go in there."

She glanced from him to the money. "Vano, I—"

"Look, Sissy—"

"Don't call me that."

"Okay, Velvet. You think you got this?"

"They're not going to want me to sign anything or read anything?"

"Just make sure the receipt matches the deposit amount. Can you do that?"

"I'm not stupid, Vano. I can read numbers, just not... words very well."

"I know you're not stupid, Vee."

"Sometimes I think you like that I can't read. Just like Pop. Gives you some control or something."

"That's not true. I never wanted to keep you out of school. That was all Pop."

"And sometimes you're just like him." She snatched the slip and deposit bag out of his hand.

"Velvet, it's just the way things have always been, you know that."

She didn't want to hear any more of his excuses, so she stormed off, snatching her purse up as she passed.

***

Vano stood in the doorway of his office and watched her go. She was wrong; he'd hated the old ways as much as she had growing up, but their old man had ruled the family with an iron fist until the day he died. And there was little he could do to go against his pop. He knew the life had been much better for him than it had been for Velvet back then because the ways of the gypsies gave little power to women. They kept the home and raised the children, and the men in the family made all the decisions. That was just the way it had always been.

Even when the old man died, things changed little. Ma ran things until Vano was of age to take over. He'd tried to take care of Velvet, but he'd gotten arrested and put in prison for several years, and rather than live another minute under Ma's control, Velvet had run off.

Well, he'd tracked her down and brought her back, like he'd sworn to Ma he'd do, and he'd made sure to eliminate all her options in the process.

She had to come back to the fold; he'd given her little choice and that wasn't by accident. And now he was determined she wouldn't have the means to run ever again.

The rear door opened, and Skin and Weasel strolled in. Not their real names—the ones they'd gone by in prison where he'd met them.

"Told you to call first. You can't just stroll in

anymore. Not with my sister working here. She don't know shit about you two, and I want to keep it that way."

"Why'd you bring her in here in the first place? She's just attracting attention and that's the last thing we need."

"I needed some way to show why our profits just went up drastically, dumbass. It's easy to explain the big draw is her."

Skin grabbed a fistful of his shirt and pinned him to the wall. "Call me dumbass again, I'll remind you of what you were in Statesville, you little shit."

"Okay, chill out."

Skin released him with a shove. "Fucking punk."

CHAPTER ELEVEN

Liam turned his truck into the parking lot of the animal shelter. As usual, there were barely any cars. He slammed the gearshift in park and climbed out. The bell over the door jingled as he walked inside, and the sound of barking dogs carried from the back. He strolled to the counter.

Pam Oswald greeted him with a smile. "Boy, am I glad to see you."

Pam was a cheerful, but overworked woman with a good heart. She was in her sixties, and Liam wondered how much longer she'd be able to keep this place going. She'd devoted her retirement and a good amount of her savings into opening this no-kill shelter, and it was always at capacity. Liam had found the place when he'd come across a stray and wanted to see if it was micro-chipped.

He'd met Pam, and she'd corralled him into helping the rest of that afternoon and coming back the following Sunday. Ever since, he'd been a regular, donating his time whenever he could.

"I had a couple hours before the shop opens. Thought I'd see if you needed some help."

"Sure do. We're short handed today. You want to let the big breeds out in the exercise yard for me?"

"Sure thing, darlin'. You know the big dogs are my favorite."

She winked at him. "A special one came in last night. Just made for all that land out at your brother's place."

He grinned. "You know I moved out. I'm in town now."

"Yeah, but Max's son, Ben, would sure love this one," she brazenly suggested, which was totally her way.

"That so, huh?"

She lifted her chin toward the back. "See for yourself. White pit bull mix with the sweetest face you ever saw."

Liam chuckled at her salesmanship and went through the swinging door to the back. He walked down the row, greeting all the other dogs until he came to the one Pam had mentioned. It was huddled against the wall of the cage. Liam let the other dogs into the exercise yard, and then returned to the new guy on the block. Liam squatted down and called it over with a soft clicking sound.

The dog shook, but its tail wagged a couple of times.

Liam could tell it was young, not a puppy, but probably no more than six months old. As he squatted there, Pam joined him, and he glanced up. "No chip?"

"Nope. Someone left him tied to the door handle. Found him when I opened up this morning.

"Some people are real pieces of shit."

"I couldn't agree more." She dug in her pocket and held out a handful of treats. "These should get him to come to you."

Liam took the offering and opened the cage door. He tossed one toward the dog. It wasn't long before his nose twitched as he sniffed the air and leaned closer to the treat. He crept toward it and gobbled it up. Liam tossed another one at half the distance and watched the dog wag its tail and hesitantly creep to it, all the time keeping watchful eyes on Liam.

This time Liam held out his palm with the remaining treats. "You're gonna have to come say hello if you want more, Buddy."

The dog sniffed the air and eyed the treats in Liam's palm, stretching his neck out. He crept closer and soon had his snout in Liam's hand. Liam ran a gentle palm down his flank. "Good boy."

Soon the dog was rubbing against Liam and licking his face.

Liam looked up at Pam who was shaking her head and smiling. "You've got the touch, son. Like no one I've ever seen."

"I don't know about that, but he does seem sweet."

She passed him a lead and gestured down the aisle. "Take him outside and work with him for a few minutes. See if he'd make a good dog for an eight-year-old boy."

Liam clipped the lead around the dog's neck and stood, his knees cracking. "Come on, buddy."

The dog followed at his side, eager to be out of the cage. When they stepped into the sunshine and fresh air, his tail wagged as he sniffed the breeze.

Liam worked with him for almost half an hour before he made his decision and brought him back into the reception area.

Pam turned from what she was doing, her eyes falling to the dog at Liam's side. "Well, I see you didn't return him to his cage. Does that mean you're taking him?"

"I'll drive him out to our place, talk to Max, let him decide if he wants Ben to meet the dog when he gets home from school. I can't make any promises."

Pam nodded. "Good deal. I'll keep my fingers crossed and hope this sweet boy finds a home."

"I better get going if I'm going to get out there and back before the shop opens."

"They want him, bring him back, and I'll micro-chip him."

"Will do."

She bent down and rubbed the dog's ears. "Good luck, boy. Be on your best behavior."

Liam led the dog outside and opened the door to his truck. The dog hopped up eagerly, sat on the seat, and stared out the windshield. Liam chuckled. "Guess you're anxious to go, huh, Buddy?"

Twenty minutes later, the pickup rolled slowly up the gravel drive to the place Liam had grown up. The old farmhouse was where Max, his wife Malee, their adoptive son Ben, and Mrs. Larsen their cook and Ben's part-time caregiver lived. Off to the left was the big new place Jameson had built for his wife Ava and their newborn daughter.

Until recently Liam had lived in the old place with Max and their youngest brother, Rory, who was rarely home anymore. When Max had married, Liam had felt it best he give them space. Especially now that Max's little family was growing even more with the news that Malee was pregnant.

Even though they'd insisted he didn't need to move out, that the farmhouse had always been just as much his as his brothers', he'd needed space of his own. Being in town, in his own place had felt like the right move. He didn't regret the decision; he still visited, often coming for Sunday dinners or bonfires.

He parked and got out. "Come on, Buddy."

The dog jumped down and sniffed around. Liam let him investigate for a few minutes. The phone in his pocket went off, and he answered it.

"Hi, it's me. How's your day going?" Velvet's soft voice filled his ear

"Hi, babe! Good. I'm out at my brother's place."

"Oh, should I let you go?"

"No. What's up?"

"Nothing. I miss you already."

Liam grinned at her admission, his eyes on the horizon. "I miss you, too. You're still coming over tonight, right?"

"Um, I don't know if I can."

His smile faded. "Why's that?"

"I may be working late. Sometimes they don't close up on time."

"Try please."

"I'll see what I can do."

Liam got the feeling she was trying to back out. "I need to see you again, Velvet. Don't you want that, too?"

"More than anything."

"I can come pick you up. They'll have to let you leave then."

"No. That's okay. I'll figure a way."

"You gonna get in trouble?"

The screen door on the front porch creaked.

"No. It'll be fine. See you tonight."

"Okay, babe. Call me when you're leaving."

"Okay. Bye."

Liam slid his phone back in his hip pocket and glanced up to see Max coming outside. He was shirtless, in a pair of sweatpants, and barefoot, a mug of coffee in his hand. "Mornin'."

"Mornin'. You get a dog?" Max ambled down the stairs. The dog sniffed his leg, and Max squatted down to scratch his ears.

"He was dumped off at the shelter last night. Left tied to the door."

"What a shit thing to do." Max scratched under the dog's jaw. "He's a sweet thing, huh?"

"Pam thought he might be a good fit for Ben." Liam didn't see any point in pussyfooting around the subject.

"Ben?" Max's brows rose.

"Doesn't every kid his age need a dog? And you sure got the space out here. This dog would be in heaven."

"Man, I don't know, Liam. A dog's a big responsibility, and with the baby on the way…"

"I understand. Just thought I'd give it a shot."

Max continued to rub the dog's chest. "He sure is a beaut."

"You wanna talk to Malee about it? Might give Ben a friend to play with out here, make him not feel so pushed aside when the new baby comes."

Max glared up at him. "He'd never be pushed aside."

"I get that, but bro, you and I both know what it's like when the new baby comes home. You with me, and me with Rory."

Max patted the dog's side and then stood, grinning.

"Yeah, Jameson and I tried to put you in a basket and leave you out in the yard. If Mom hadn't caught us goin' out the back door you would've been wolf bait."

"Very funny."

Max took a sip of coffee and lifted the mug. "You want a cup?"

"Thought you'd never ask."

"Since when do I have to ask? You always just walk in."

Liam shrugged. "You got a wife now."

"Yeah, so?"

"She's knocked up. All those hormones... I don't want to piss her off."

"Shut up and bring your dog." Max headed toward the porch.

Liam grinned and followed. "Not my dog, he's your dog. And his name's Buddy."

CHAPTER TWELVE

Velvet woke up against Liam's warm muscled body. Warm was putting it mildly; the man was like an inferno. She lifted her head from his chest and let her eyes travel over his naked body. She moved and felt the soreness between her thighs that would remind her all day long how much sex they'd had last night.

He'd teased and tormented her, but now it was her turn. She slid down the sheet and moved between his legs. She looked up at him carefully; he had one arm thrown up on the pillow, his other hand rested on his stomach.

She gently touched his cock, stroking it to life. It didn't take long, and she ran her tongue up it then took him into her mouth.

***

Liam cracked an eye and looked down, his hand automatically fisting in the silky hair that spread over his stomach. Velvet's mouth sank down over his dick again, and he moaned, clenching tight. His other hand came up to gather her hair in his hands and hold it from her face. He wanted to be able to watch his dick, wet and glistening, pump in and out of her sweet mouth. It had played a big part in the fantasies he'd had of her in the weeks since LA. Especially as he stood in his shower, his hand on his soap covered dick, imagining her pouty red lips wrapped around him and moaning as he took her.

He pumped his hips up, holding her still with his hands in her hair. She moaned around him, but her mouth moved quicker up and down until he felt his release creep up on him. He pulled free and dragged her up the bed, and in one fluid motion, he flipped her onto her stomach and yanked her ass up in the air, pushing her shoulders to the mattress.

He clenched her hips tight and buried himself in her soaked pussy.

She gasped and squirmed, but his hold was unbreakable as he controlled the pace. With this angle, his thrusts could go deeper, and he knew they dragged over her g-spot with each pump.

He kept one hand locked on her hip but dipped the other to toy with her clit. He could feel the pulses of her pussy clenching around him. He ached to his balls with the need to pound into her, but he wanted to get her there first. He stared down at her perfect heart shaped ass and couldn't help but pop it with a smack.

She sucked in a breath and shattered into orgasm, coming so hard for him, his restraint snapped. All it took was the image burned in his brain of her mouth on his cock and he exploded, slamming home and shooting into her. "Fuck!"

He pulled her up on her knees, still hard inside her. She moaned as his hands closed over her breasts, and he pinched her nipples hard. She whimpered and clenched down on his dick again.

"Yes, baby. God, I love that," he growled. "You take me so good."

He lowered them both gently to the bed and gathered her in his arms. He stroked his calloused hands over the soft skin of her back, down to her ass and up again, over and over.

***

Velvet cuddled against Liam, enjoying his gentle touch until he broke the silence.

"Babe?"

"Hmm?"

"What's your real name?"

She bit her lip, hesitating before answering. She

lifted her head from his chest. "It's a stupid name. I hate it."

"Come on. It can't be that bad."

"Veleena."

Liam tried to stifle his grin. "I was wrong."

She smacked him on the shoulder. "Jerk."

"Sorry. It's a real...pretty name. But Velvet suits you better." He ran his hand up her arm. "Velvet. The word just makes me want to touch your skin."

She rolled to her back and took his hand, guiding it slowly up her chest, the whole while her eyes locked with his. It was all the invitation he needed. He lowered his mouth to hers and moved over her again.

"Damn, woman. You're insatiable."

"You made me this way."

An hour later, after they'd gone another round and recovered, he smacked her ass. "Come on, pretty girl. We've got places to go."

Once they were dressed, Velvet grabbed her sling bag and tied her pullover jacket around her waist. Liam locked up the place and they skipped down the stairs. He tugged her into the bakery. Mrs. Heinzlemann greeted him with a smile and soon they had coffee and warm pastries in hand. As he was paying, she passed him a paper bag, smiling and nodding at Velvet.

"Schöne Frau."

He grabbed it and winked at her. "Ja."

Velvet couldn't help her curiosity as they walked out of the shop. "What did she say to you?"

"She said you were a beautiful woman."

Velvet grinned. "I knew I liked her."

Liam chuckled.

"So you speak German?"

"Don't be too impressed. I only know a little."

She gobbled the pastry down and made a grab for the bag, but he held it out of reach.

"Na uh."

"What's in the bag? It smells delicious."

"I had her pack us some sandwiches for lunch. You'll have to wait."

Liam stopped at a motorcycle parked at a spot half a block down, and Velvet's eyes swept over it. It was backed into the spot, its rear tire to the curb. It was slung low and long with gleaming black paint and shining chrome pipes. "This is yours?"

"Yep." He shoved the last of his pastry in his mouth and licked his thumb.

"I didn't know you rode."

"Been riding since I was in high school." He drank down his coffee, tossed it in a trashcan on the curb, and then tucked the sack into his saddlebag. He jerked his chin at her sling bag. "You want me to put that in here?"

"Sure." She passed it to him. Once he had it tucked away, he took two helmets out of the other saddlebag and handed her one.

"You ever ridden before?" he asked, strapping his on and slipping a pair of sunglasses over his eyes. He stepped to her, carefully pulling the shades she had pushed up on her head down over her eyes.

She grinned at his attentiveness. "No, I've never been on one."

He leaned down and brushed his lips against hers, drawing her hips forward until she was flush against him. When he lifted his head, he asked, "You okay with taking the bike? If not, we can take my truck."

She found it sweet that he would ask, wanting her to be comfortable with this. She stepped back and put the helmet on her head. "I want to ride."

"My kind of girl." He buckled the strap under her chin and moved to the motorcycle. Throwing his leg over the seat, he lifted the heavy bike off its kickstand and fired it up. It roared to life with the unmistakable rumble of a Harley. He looked back at her and jerked his chin. "Climb on, darlin'."

She did without hesitation, pressing close against his back and wrapping her arms around him.

"You good?" he asked over his shoulder.

When she nodded, he pulled out and they roared down the street. Her exhilaration factor went from zero to off the charts in two-point-six seconds, and she couldn't keep from grinning. Everything was different riding down the street on the bike. She felt the wind on her face and the power of the bike under her. She had an unobstructed view of the scenery around her; it was totally different than riding in a vehicle.

He stopped at a light a few blocks down and put his boots down on the pavement, then patted her thigh with his left hand. "You good?"

"This is awesome!"

He chuckled. "That's my girl."

The light changed, and they roared off.

Soon they were riding down Interstate 70 and headed up into the mountains. They rode for about twenty minutes before Liam exited and made a left turn down a dirt road. Velvet had never been up into the mountains around here, and she couldn't help being in awe of the beauty all around her. Still, she wondered where they were going. About a mile down the road, she had her answer; he turned again at a small sign that read *Wild Horse Refuge*.

There was a closed metal gate. He stopped the bike, and they climbed off. She was surprised when he walked over, opened the gate, and rolled the bike through. "What are you doing? Are we supposed to be here?"

"Yeah. The gate isn't to keep us out; it's to keep the horses and foals from wandering off the protected area."

They rode the bike farther up the dirt trail several miles, its engine rumbling quietly. Liam finally coasted to a stop where the dirt road split. He dug out Velvet's sling bag, the paper bag, and some bottles of water and shoved them into a nylon backpack. He stowed their helmets, but they kept the sunglasses. Slipping the pack on his back, he held his hand out to her. "Come on."

She took it and they walked a trail that followed along a creek bed. Velvet was in awe of the rugged scenery all around them. "How big is this place?"

"Thirty-six thousand acres. Made up mostly of rocky canyons and plateaus. This entrance isn't too steep, though. We'll follow the creek bed. It's not too far of a hike in. There's one hill at the beginning, then we'll continue on a fairly flat wash for a long while."

"You've been here before?"

"Once, a long time ago."

"And there are wild horses here?"

"Yes, ma'am."

"Then I'm glad I brought my camera."

He turned to smile at her. "Is that why that bag is so heavy?"

She grinned back. "Yep."

"You like to take pictures?" he asked as they walked.

She shrugged. "It's kind of a hobby, nothing serious."

"And what *are* you serious about?"

She huffed out a laugh. "I don't think anyone has ever asked me that."

"There must be something."

"There is. I'm just not sure I want to share it."

He looked over at her. "Hmm. Mysterious."

"Not really, just… I wouldn't want you to laugh."

"Why would I laugh?"

She shrugged.

They walked along the trail in silence for a few

steps before he stopped and turned her to him. "Velvet, I promise I won't laugh." And then he did the one thing that was her undoing. He made an X over his chest. "Cross my heart."

And with those three little words and that gesture, she was a fifteen-year-old girl again, asking him to promise to do right by her tattoo. She started to get choked up and was afraid he would see it and think she was crazy for getting so emotional. So she fought off the feeling with a flippant reply, turning to walk again. "Fine. Whatever. It's no big deal."

He fell in beside her. "Then tell me."

"I want to open a coffee shop."

"Really?"

"Yes. A quaint little vintage coffee shop with multi-paned windows like an old English shop. And there'd be a fireplace and books to read—lots of books, shelves full of them, and a little corner for children with a colorful rug for them to lay on and read while their parents sip my amazing coffee drinks."

He huffed out a soft laugh. "Wow."

She came to an abrupt stop, whirling on him. "You find it funny? The tatted-up girl wants to do something so… so vanilla and mundane? Oh, the irony of it, huh?" There was more irony to it than that, if he only knew she couldn't even read, he'd be laughing his ass off. She stalked off, but he grabbed her arm, stopping her.

"Wait a damn minute. That's not what I was thinking. You could never be vanilla, Velvet. Not in a million years."

"I saw your reaction."

"I'm in awe, is all. You have it worked out, down to the last detail. Hell, I can practically see the place in my head."

"Really?" She stared intently at him. It would mean the world to her if he liked her idea.

He chuckled. "I can even smell the coffee." He took in a deep breath. "And it smells delicious."

She giggled and shook her head, looking down to kick a stone. "You're delusional. And teasing me."

"I'd go to a place like that."

That brought her head up. "You would?"

"Hell, yeah. I think a lot of people would go there." He took her hand and began walking again. "I think Grand Junction could really use a place like that."

She stared at the ground. She'd never thought of settling permanently in Grand Junction and certainly never imagined opening her coffee shop there.

"I'd love to do whatever I can to help you make it happen."

No one had ever offered to help her. "Are you serious?"

"Serious as a heart attack, lady."

"Thanks, but... Well, for now it's just a dream. It was a goal I thought I'd gotten close to but..."

"But what? I thought your calendar was selling well."

"It was. It did phenomenal."

"You didn't make enough to get started?"

"I..." She paused, hesitant to admit she'd been swindled.

"Velvet?" He stopped her again.

She took a deep breath and blurted it out. "I had a location all lined up. I was this close to signing the lease and putting up the money. But it all fell through."

"How? Why?"

"My photographer took off with all the profits."

"You're shittin' me."

"Nope."

"Son-of-a-bitch, sweetheart. I'm sorry. How much did he take?"

"Fifteen grand. It would have been almost

enough."

"I'm so sorry."

"I shouldn't have trusted him."

"Why?"

She just shook her head. "I keep getting used."

He searched her face. "Let's find him and kick his ass."

"He's disappeared and changed his number. I tried contacting the woman he was dating, but she says he broke up with her just after the show, and she hasn't seen him." She realized she was really bringing the mood of the day down. Shrugging, she shook it off and continued walking. "Spilt milk. Nothing I can do about it now."

"So that's why you're working at House of Ink? You needed a job?"

"It was the first thing that came along. It's just until I can get some modeling jobs lined up or something." She hadn't told him that her brother owned the shop and didn't plan to admit it now.

"I see. So you won't be staying in town?"

He sounded almost heartbroken. She smiled and bumped shoulders with him. "I'm finding more and more reasons to stay."

"I aim to be one of them."

"You are."

"Good."

He looked happy again and she liked seeing that.

"You'll get through this, Velvet. The modeling jobs will start rolling in, and we can get you another photographer—one with ethics. I'm sure Jameson knows someone."

"I suppose." Glancing over, she saw only honest caring and concern, not any motive to get something from her like so many men in her past. And for just a moment she wondered if she should tell him her other secrets—about not being able to read, about her brother owning the shop, and most importantly about who her family was and the con on Brothers Ink of which she'd taken part. Would he understand?

Harsh reality descended. No, of course he wouldn't; he *couldn't*. No normal person could understand what that kind of life was like, and there was no way he'd ever be able to forgive her.

Still, something inside her, perhaps some self-sabotaging mechanism, wanted to throw all her cards on the table and see if he really did care. To stop herself from the temptation to blurt out the truth, she turned the tables on him. "How about you?"

"How about me what?"

"I shared something personal. Now you share something about you."

"I hate snakes."

"That's not very personal."

"It is when I come across one."

"Come on, be serious. Who is Liam O'Rourke?"

He cocked his head, considering. "Hmm. Well, I'm very protective, soft-hearted, hard-headed, and a smartass."

"Really? What else?"

"I can be blunt, hedonistic, impatient, and a little OCD."

"Wow. You're a mess," she teased.

He chuckled. "Yep. Sound like a real catch, don't I?"

She laughed with him. "The body makes up for it."

"Oh, really?"

"Now tell me something serious. Something you haven't shared with anyone."

He stared off at the horizon a moment, and then admitted, "Rory says I'm afraid to take a risk with people."

"And you believe him, why?"

"It's probably true."

She frowned. "Why are you afraid?"

He shrugged. "I don't know."

"Yes, you do."

His eyes came to hers, searching. "My parents died when I was in my early teens. I've been sort of closed off since then."

"I'm so sorry. What happened?"

"Car accident. Jameson was supposed to head off to college that fall. He gave that up, got a job, and raised us all."

"It must have been very hard for all of you."

He nodded. "Max struggled with a lot of anger, started getting into street fights, eventually found a place called Pops' Gym and took up boxing. That straightened him out. Me? I just sort of closed down and stopped caring about much of anything. Jameson got me working at the shop right out of high school, taught me everything I know. I just sort of put myself into that."

"You're like me. Afraid of getting hurt, of losing one more thing…"

He studied her and finally nodded. "Yeah, I suppose so."

She looked away. She wanted more than anything in that moment to be able to assure him she would never hurt him, but that would be a lie. If and when he found out the truth about her, it would hurt him deeply.

"You're the first person I've ever thought was worth the risk, Velvet."

Her eyes stung with unshed tears. God, she didn't want to hurt him. He was everything she ever wanted in a man, and perhaps if things had been different, if she'd never walked into Brothers Ink all those years ago—

"I admire the way you're not afraid to go for it."

Maybe that was true everywhere else in her life, but it wasn't the case where he was concerned. Here in this moment she was terrified to go for what she really wanted. Blinking away the moisture in her eyes, she tried to laugh it off. "Thanks, that means a lot. So, tell me, Liam, do you like what you do?"

"What, tattooing?"

She nodded.

"I do."

"What else do you like?"

"Rock climbing, working with strays at the shelter, and old school vinyl albums."

"Vinyl, that's cool. Do you collect them?"

"I have a few."

She grinned. "Why do I feel like that's an understatement?"

"Okay, more than a few."

"Tell me about the animal shelter."

He shrugged. "I found a stray once, took it in to see if it had a microchip. Pam runs the place; she kind of roped me into helping out. Now I go down there whenever I get time. She's a great lady… really cares about the animals. You'll have to come out to my brother's place and see the sweet pup I just took there for his son, Ben. Max says those two hit it off right away. Buddy even slept on Ben's bed last night."

"I'd love to meet them." She tucked her hand in his arm. "So, Pam at the shelter, Mrs. Heinzlemann down at the bakery, seems like this whole town loves you." That was something she longed for—to belong and be accepted by the community rather than be shunned and hated like her family had been. She was self-aware enough to know that was probably what the dream of the coffee shop was all about—gaining that love and acceptance.

"It wasn't always that way. There was a time when people in town didn't think too much of us. Four boys growing up without parents, running loose on the town with just an eighteen-year-old as the head of the household, and one that took up tattooing as the way to support us all. No, it wasn't that way at all."

"What changed?"

"Jameson became famous when he was asked to do a reality show. Suddenly he was the town's favorite son. Funny how fame works. Guess it made people give us a chance. They got to see our personalities on TV and that we weren't something to be feared, that we weren't some lowlife criminals or something."

Which was exactly what they would think of her.

A chipmunk scurried across their path, and they reached the top of a rise. Velvet's eyes were on the loose gravel and stone, not wanting to lose her footing when Liam grabbed her forearm. She glanced up, and he had his finger over his mouth indicating she should stay quiet. He lifted his chin toward the distance.

There, partway up on the side of the canyon was a horse. It was black and white, painted like one she imagined a Native American would have ridden in the old west. It stood out against the brown landscape.

"Oh my God," Velvet whispered.

"And look over there," Liam murmured. Her eyes followed his gaze, and she spotted a buckskin-colored mare and foal.

"This is amazing! Quick, give me my camera."

Liam slipped the pack off his wide shoulders and quietly unzipped it. He passed her bag to her, and she pulled out her Nikon. She popped off the lens cap and put it to her eye, adjusting the focus.

She clicked away, flipping the camera back and forth and shifting to get different angles.

To their right, there was a nicker from a very close distance. They both turned to see a big chestnut stallion with a black mane and tail. It stood proudly staring at them from just twenty yards away.

"Wow," was all Velvet could say.

"He's a beauty. Must stand fifteen hands high. Just stay still," Liam murmured.

The stallion tossed his head.

"He's posing for you, babe."

Velvet brought the camera up and zoomed in for a great shot. These were going to be amazing; she couldn't wait to print them.

After a few minutes, the horse trotted off.

Liam grabbed her arm. "Come on."

They followed the stallion for a while, and Velvet got a lot more photos. He didn't seem to care that they were there. Eventually he moved off down the canyon to the others.

Liam gestured to some flat rocks. "Let's sit."

The rocks were warm from the sun that had now climbed high in the sky. Liam dug in his pack and took out the paper bag containing the sandwiches. He passed one to her along with a bottle of water.

Velvet unwrapped hers and took a big bite, then moaned around the mouthful. When she swallowed it down, she declared, "Best sandwich ever!"

Liam smiled and put a water bottle to his mouth, tilted it up, and guzzled it. She watched the muscles in his neck work. He really was quite handsome.

He caught her watching and set the half-empty bottle down on the rock between them. "You having a good time?"

She looked out at the view. "I'm have a wonderful time. It's gorgeous up here. Thank you for bringing me. Seeing wild horses like that… It was amazing. I'd have to say this is the most unique experience I've ever had."

"Good. I'm glad you like it up here. Not everyone is the outdoor type."

Her brows rose. "You mean not every *girl* is the outdoor type."

He chuckled. "Yeah, that's what I meant."

"Um hmm." She cocked her head at him. "Was this a test?"

"No."

"It so totally was." She smacked his shoulder.

"I admit nothing." He chuckled, finished the last bite of his sandwich, and looked over at her. "But, since you passed, maybe we could go camping one night up at Dominguez Canyon."

"Ah ha! It was a test!"

He grinned, not confirming.

"Where's Dominguez Canyon?"

"It's not far, but it's in the other direction. It's even prettier than this place."

She scanned the landscape. "Not possible."

"It is so possible."

She turned to him, tilting her chin up. "You'll have to prove that to me, mister."

"You're on, lady."

They ate in silence, occasionally glancing over at each other. When Velvet was through, she tucked the trash in the pack. The wind picked up, and she untied the jacket from her waist, slipping it over her head.

Liam squinted up at the ridge of gray clouds blowing across the sky. "We should head back. Wouldn't want to get caught out here if the bottom falls out of those clouds. These dry gullies carry all the water down the canyon."

She nodded and stood, brushing off her pants. "You're right. I'm glad we got as much time as we did. I think I got some fantastic shots. I can't wait to print and frame them."

"I'd love to see them."

"I'll give you copies."

By the time they made it back to the bike, the wind had really picked up. Liam got them quickly to the interstate, and they skirted around the storm. Large dark swaths of rain trailed to the ground from the clouds on the horizon.

When they arrived in Grand Junction, Liam parked at Brothers Ink.

"You want to see our shop?" he asked. "I'd like you to meet my brothers."

"Sure," she replied, knowing she'd have to pretend she'd never been in the place before. She looked different than she did back then, with her dark hair and colored contacts, but she still worried Jameson would somehow recognize her as the teenage girl whose mother had shaken him down for a thousand dollar payoff.

They walked hand in hand into the shop.

CHAPTER THIRTEEN

A muscular man stood at the counter, talking with a customer when they walked in. Velvet assumed he must be one of Liam's brothers.

"I put a copy of the care instructions we went over in the bag with the cleanser. If you have questions, please don't hesitate to call us."

The woman took the bag. "I will. And thanks again. I love the tattoo."

He grinned at her, flashing beautiful white teeth. "You're welcome, Tina. I'm glad you're happy with it."

After the woman exited the front door, Liam's hand landed on Velvet's back, guiding her forward. "Velvet, this is my older brother, Maxwell. Max, this is Velvet Jones."

Max extended his hand, but his question was for Liam. "This the woman you met in LA?"

"Yes, she is." Liam smiled down at her.

"Well, you certainly made an impression on my brother, Ms. Jones."

"Please, call me Velvet."

"Velvet. I wasn't at the expo, but I heard you had quite a following, lines down the aisle, Liam said."

She let out a soft laugh. "We did sell a lot of calendars."

"Welcome to town. Liam says you're working over at House of Ink. So, are you an artist as well as a model?"

"I…uh, know the owner. I was sort of between jobs, and he needed some help running the shop. But, no, I'm not a tattoo artist. I've always admired those who are; I think it takes a lot of skill to do it well."

"Yes, well, not sure how much skill there is over at House of— "

"Max." Liam cut him off with a warning.

"Anyway, welcome to our humble shop, m'lady." Maxwell took a deep bow, and Velvet curtsied in return.

"Kind sir."

"And that's my little brother, Rory." Liam lifted his chin toward another man bent over the customer sitting in his chair. He had long dark hair and a short beard around his mouth. He glanced up and gave her a smile.

"Hey, lady."

She returned his grin, and he went back to inking

his customer.

Max leaned on the counter, his hands clasped. "So what have you two been up to?"

Liam hooked his arm around her and pulled her close. "Took a ride up to see the wild horses."

"Book Cliff?" Max's brows rose. "What did you think of it?"

She smiled brightly at him. "It was amazing. One came right up by us, then let us follow behind him for a while. I got some great shots."

"I'd love to see them," Max said.

She dug in her bag and took out her camera. The three of them leaned in.

"Those are fantastic," Maxwell agreed.

"Here's my favorite." She found the close-up of the stallion's profile. It was staring off, the wind blowing through its mane. She turned the screen to let them both see it.

Liam studied the shot and met her eyes. "It kind of reminds me of you…wild and beautiful."

"That would make an awesome tattoo," Max suggested.

She gazed down at the shot. "It would, wouldn't it?"

"Let me do it. Put that on you," Liam

murmured.

Her eyes flashed up, and her mouth parted. She'd dreamed of Liam inking her skin again, ever since the day he'd first worked on her.

Max lifted his chin at Liam. "If you want it done, Liam's the man for that kind of work. His realism is amazing. It would look phenomenal in black and gray shading."

And just like that she knew she had to have him tattoo this on her. "Will you do it?"

His eyes moved from her to Max and back. "You sure about this? I don't want you to let Max talk you into it."

"I'm sure. Can you do it today? Now?"

His brows rose. "Now?"

"I mean, if you have time. If you want to do it."

Max answered for him with a big grin. "Oh, sweetheart if he didn't have time, which he does since he took the day off to spend with you, he would make the time. I'm sure he'd like nothing more than to lay ink on your skin. Hell, he's probably fantasized about it."

She couldn't keep the smile off her face. She cocked a brow at Liam, the thought thrilling her. "Is that true?"

He stared down into her face and confessed,

"Maybe."

Max let out a huff of a laugh. "Maybe? That's a load of bullshit."

"Okay," Liam glared at Max, then back to her, "I'll admit it. I have thought about what it would be like, yeah."

Max chuckled and held his arm out. "Right this way, m'lady. His station is the first on the left."

Velvet moved past Liam to his chair. The first thing she noticed was her calendar stuck up on his mirror. "You bought one!"

"Yeah, me and every other guy there that night."

She frowned. "But I don't remember seeing you in the line."

"That's because I got it for him." Rory looked up from his client. "Liam wanted to meet you, but he was tied up watching our booth."

Velvet nodded, gazing up at Liam. "If you had come through the line, I definitely would have remembered you." In more ways than one. He would have stood out in the line just for his rugged good looks, but she would have recognized him. Perhaps it was best he hadn't. If he had, she may have been so shocked she'd have given it all away.

Liam sat on the rolling stool next to her. He took the camera from her. "I'll do a sketch."

While he worked, she secretly ran her fingertips over the tattoo on the inside of her left arm. It was the one he had already given her so many years ago. As she did, her excitement to have him ink her again grew.

***

Jameson leaned back in his chair and looked at the man who sat across his desk. "We finished, Ryan?"

The man clicked off the recording. "I think I've got enough for the article. Thanks for your time."

"Always happy to get coverage in Inked Up magazine. You guys have been really good to me. Helped my career immensely in the early days."

"You deserve it. There's just one more thing we need to decide on."

"What's that?"

"The cover shot. We could do a close up of you inking, or you at your desk, or—"

Jameson rolled his eyes. "You know the place is called Brothers Ink for a reason. There are four of us. How about we get a shot of all of us?"

"I suppose that would work." He stood. "I'll get the photographer's ideas. We want to come back for that end of the month. That work for you?"

"I'll make it work, just let me know the date. Come on, I'll walk you out."

They descended the stairs and walked through the shop, pausing to watch as Liam laughed intimately with a woman as he showed her a sketch. She nodded excitedly, and he leaned in to give her a kiss. Her hands cupped his face, and she pressed her body to his. They broke the kiss and pressed foreheads together.

"That's some crazy chemistry those two have got going." Ryan turned to Jameson. "I think we've got our cover models."

Jameson grinned. "I agree."

"Cover models?" Liam asked, turning his attention from the woman.

"Liam, this is Ryan Kelly. He's with Inked Up. They're doing an article on the shop. We were just discussing what to put on the cover."

They shook hands.

"And I recognize this lady," Ryan said, smiling at Velvet. He shook her hand. "Velvet Jones. Nice to finally meet you."

"You, too."

"So you want us for the cover of Inked Up?" Liam asked, his eyes going between the reporter and Jameson.

"You two have crazy hot chemistry. I think we could get some amazing shots."

Liam looked at Velvet. "Here's that next modeling job you were waiting for, babe. You in?"

"Only if I get to do all the shots with you."

"Done," said Ryan.

"How much does this gig pay?" Liam asked.

"Three hundred for her. Nothing for you since your shop's the subject of the article."

"I'll do it," Velvet said.

Ryan pulled a business card out of his pocket and handed it to her. "Call me, and we'll work out the details. We're looking to shoot at the end of the month. That work for you?"

"Whenever you want. I'll make sure I'm available."

"Great. Nice to meet you, Ms. Jones." He turned and shook Jameson's hand. "I'll be in touch."

"Safe travels, Ryan. Good to see you again."

***

When he'd left, Velvet turned to Liam, her mouth open. "They want us on the cover!"

"Told you things would turn around. Maybe the photographer they send will be interested in shooting another calendar."

Her brows shot up. "That would be amazing."

Jameson stuck out his hand. "We haven't officially met. I'm Liam's older brother, Jameson."

"Nice to meet you. Of course with your reputation in the industry, I've heard so much about you."

"I heard you were going to be in LA, but unfortunately I couldn't make the expo. So, you're in Grand Junction permanently now?"

"Well, I…" Her eyes shifted to Liam. "I'm not sure for how long, but I do like it here."

"Well, it's nice to have you in town." He looked at Liam. "You going to let Liam do some work on you?"

"I am, yeah." He held the sketch up. "Check out the photograph."

Velvet held up the camera, and he leaned in. "Wow. Great shot. This from up at Book Cliff?"

Liam nodded. "We rode up there this morning."

"It was amazing," Velvet added.

"Well, I'll let you get to it." Jameson squeezed his brother's shoulder. "Nice meeting you, Velvet."

When he left, Liam looked at her. "Do you know where you want it?"

"Um…"

"I have the perfect spot. Right between your shoulder blades, between the scrollwork that runs down both sides." He dipped his head. "I'll be able to see it every time I take you from behind."

She blushed, glancing to see if his brothers had overheard.

Liam teased her. "Well, my, my… The brazen Velvet Jones can blush."

"Shut. Up."

He chuckled again. "So how about it?"

She nodded.

He patted his hand on the flat padded table. "Face down, baby girl."

CHAPTER FOURTEEN

Monday morning Velvet arrived at House of Ink an hour before opening time, unlocking the back door and heading toward the restroom. She paused when she heard voices coming from her brother's office. He was still at the house, so who was here? She stood in the shadow of the hallway, listening at the crack in the door. Two men inside were talking. She could only see one of them, a bald man with an earring and tattoos running up his arm; the other man was out of sight. The one she could see had a laptop and was scrolling through social media sites, scanning information and jotting notes on a legal pad.

"This scheme of Vano's is brilliant," said the one out of sight.

"Yep." The one jotting notes picked up a phone and dialed a number. "Is this Gerald Hempstead?" There was a pause. "I'm calling about your grandson, Thomas Hempstead. I'm the public defender from Grand Junction, Colorado. Your grandson is in jail. Yes, sir. He was involved in a car accident, and he's been charged with a DUI offense. Well, sir, that means he's been arrested on drunk driving charges. As you may or may not know he already has one DUI charge on his record. Yes, sir, I do. Well, the reason I'm calling is if… Yes, sir. Thomas gave me your number. Well, if he can get this bail paid by tomorrow he can be released. He'll need $2400. Yes, sir, it is a lot of money. Let me let you talk to him."

Velvet peeked around the doorframe and saw the bald man hold out the phone, his palm covering the mouthpiece. She couldn't see who the person taking the receiver was, just the sleeve of a blue flannel shirt.

The bald man whispered to his co-conspirator, "Facebook says the boy calls him Poppy."

"Got it." The other man cleared his throat, and then in a young sounding voice whispered and sniffled, "Poppy? I was in a b-bad a-accident. I knocked my h-head really b-bad and it hurts. Can you p-please send the money so I can get out of here? O-okay. Thank you, Poppy. I love you." The phone was passed back again with a whispered, "He bought it."

"Mr. Hempstead? Yes, sir. The clerk's office doesn't take credit cards. No, sir. If you send a check, Thomas won't be released until the check clears. No, it's best to send cash. You can overnight it via FedEx to the address that I'm going to give you. Yes, sir, it's the best way to get him released quickly. He seems to be quite upset. I'd hate to see him spend the weekend in lockup. I wouldn't normally make a call like this, but I talked with your grandson, and he told me about being accepted to Yale University next fall. He seems like a good boy. Yes, sir. Here's that address."

Velvet listened to the bald man give a PO box. Soon the call ended, and the two chuckled.

"The old geezers fall for it every damn time."

"Because of the way you scripted it. Good work, man."

"Vano said you just have to target the right mark and do your research, Weasel. Make sure they're seventy or older and have grandkids old enough to be getting into trouble. Make sure they're good kids. Grandparents love their grandkids. They'll help them. Works almost every time."

"Like taking candy from a baby. What's your total for the day?"

"Hmm. Looks like I'm just shy of ten-thousand,

and that's only my third call of the morning."

"Awesome!"

"I'm gonna take a quick break." A chair creaked, and Velvet darted down the hall into the women's restroom. She closed the door silently and listened as footsteps passed by.

She pressed her back to the door and covered her mouth. Oh, my God, this was so much worse than she'd imagined. Vano was unscrupulous, yes, and he'd learned every con there was from their father, but this? Targeting the elderly? Playing on their feelings, causing them all this heartache and pain? This was just too much.

CHAPTER FIFTEEN

That night, Velvet retreated to her bedroom and tried to figure out what to do about Vano. She paced back and forth, turning over every option in her head. Her brother was raised in this life, and conning for money rather than earning it came natural for him. It was all he knew, but that didn't excuse it. He was an adult now and able to choose for himself, same as she. He knew what he was doing was wrong, and if she didn't put a stop to it, he'd suck her into his dirty dealings sooner or later. Besides, how could she live with herself if she didn't stop him?

But gypsies didn't rat on each other.

When she was younger, she'd had no choice in how her family had used her in their cons, but things were different now. She knew better; perhaps she'd always known, even at the age of seven, that what her family did was wrong.

She bit her lip. Her brother could be stern and vicious in his dealings, and he wouldn't hesitate to use whatever method he needed to in order to get her under his thumb and go along with whatever he was doing. That was the way their family was and had always been.

The men ruled the family, and whatever they said was law. Her mother had bowed in every way to their father until the day he died. It was only at his death that she took charge, and that only lasted until Vano took control when he turned twenty-one and could legally take over the finances.

The front door opened, and voices carried down the hall, jolting her from her thoughts. She pressed her ear to the door, then slowly cracked it open.

"You got anything to drink in this place?" a deep voice growled.

Velvet glanced at the clock by the bed. 11:00 PM. Her brother must have closed the shop early tonight. Hell, they hadn't had any customers all afternoon, which was why he let her leave.

"There's beer in the fridge. At least there better be. Velvet was supposed to pick some up."

"She here?"

"Nah. Said she was goin' out. She's seein' that guy from Brothers Ink."

The top popped on a can of beer. "Your sister's a

real looker."

"Don't get any ideas, Skin."

"And if I do? Who's gonna stop me? You?"

"I'm just sayin'… I don't want any problems."

"You just keep your mouth shut, Vano, and keep takin' your cut of this deal and there won't be any problems. Your sister and me… that's gonna happen. Maybe not now, but I promise you she will be mine."

"Dude, that wasn't part of the deal we made."

"I'm makin' it part, and you ain't gonna say shit about it. We know too much about you and your little schemes. Plus you owe us for takin' care of you in prison, and that bill isn't paid up until we clear a quarter million—that was the deal. This is makin' you rich, too, so shut the hell up. Understand?"

There was silence in the room, and Velvet trembled. She recognized those voices; they were the ones she'd overheard making those phone calls. She couldn't believe her brother was letting them say those things or that he wasn't throwing them out on their ass. God, what did they have on him?

"I asked you a question."

"Fine."

A deep voice chuckled. "Yeah, that's what I thought."

"I don't want her knowing anything about our deal," Vano insisted.

"She's been takin' walks down the back hall. She better not find out what we've got going on."

"She won't, Skin."

"She does, you better get her on board."

"She won't cause any problems," Vano promised.

"She does, I'm gonna break your legs and that's just for starters."

Velvet eyed the window. Could she get it up without any noise? She wanted to run to Liam's. She wanted to be wrapped in his arms and as far away from all of this as she could get.

She crossed the room and yanked on the handles, but the window in the old house was painted shut. Damn it. She moved back to the door.

"We're almost square," Vano said.

"No we ain't. You're fifty grand in the hole."

"Bullshit, Skin. Not with the fifteen grand I gave you last month."

"You mean stole from that photographer," the other man snickered.

"Shut up, Weasel. I didn't steal it. I took it."

Velvet's mouth dropped open. *Oh, my God.* Vano took her money? She could only imagine how he must have intimidated Aaron to get him to hand over her hard earned cash. She grit her teeth. *Vano, you son-of-a-bitch!*

The one he'd called Skin laughed. "Yeah, the only one here screwing over your sister is you, Vano."

"I needed that money. What does she need that kind of money for? Fucking chick would just blow it on something stupid. Anyway, she needs to get married. I'll have to start looking for a husband to marry her off to. A rich one."

"You're a piece of work. Still livin' in the dark ages. Arranged marriages? That's some bullshit," Skin said. "I'd take her, but I'm not the marryin' kind."

"I could be for that sweet ass," the other man said.

"Fuckin' shut up, Weasel. You ain't touchin' her. I already called dibs." There was a chuckle. "Sure wish she was here."

"Get your hand off your crotch, Skin."

Dibs? A chair creaked as someone stood, and she held her breath.

"Maybe we wait long enough, she'll come home. I'm gettin' another beer; you want one?" Weasel asked.

She was terrified that one or both of those men would decide to wander down the hall and check to make sure she wasn't home. She had no intention of facing them without something to skew the odds in her favor. She slowly opened her door, making sure it didn't squeak. Tiptoeing across the hall, she darted into her brother's room and pulled out the drawer of his nightstand.

"Thank you, God," she whispered, grateful for the 9mm pistol her brother always kept by his bed. She picked up the heavy weapon and darted across the hall. Then she crawled soundlessly into the back of her closet, slid down the wall to sit on the floor, and braced the gun on her knees, aiming it at the louvered doors.

She'd keep that position until morning if she had to.

CHAPTER SIXTEEN

The next morning, as she walked to work, Velvet took her phone out and dialed Aaron's number. Predictably, he didn't pick up, but unlike the last times, it went to voicemail so she left a message. "Aaron, I know it was Vano. Please call me."

Surprisingly, she didn't have long to wait. Before she made it to the shop, her phone rang. She didn't recognize the number, but she answered anyway. "Hello."

"Velvet. It's me."

"Aaron." She stopped dead in her tracks at the stoplight on the corner. She took in a slow breath, trying to hold onto her anger. "He came to see you, didn't he? My brother."

Aaron let out a huff. "Yes. Him and his two thugs."

She froze, pressing the phone closer. "Thugs? He had someone with him?"

"Scary dudes. They threatened me."

"Threatened you?"

"Well, not in so many words, but I knew if I didn't hand over the money they'd beat the shit outta me. There were three of them, Velvet. What could I do?"

"Why didn't you tell me?"

"He swore if I told you, they'd be back to deal with me. I'm sorry, Velvet, but your brother is a real asshole."

"I know. I'm sorry you got sucked into this."

"Look, I'll give you the digital files and sign over the rights if you want to print up more, maybe do another expo. But I'm done with it. I'm sorry, but I don't want anything to do with your brother. I don't need that kind of trouble."

"I understand. Thank you, Aaron. It would mean a great deal to me. It would help me get away from him."

"And you won't tell him I gave them to you?"

"You don't have to be afraid of him, Aaron. He won't be coming after you. He already got what he was after."

"You mean the money?"

"Partly, but that was just a means to an end. What he really wanted was to force me to come back here with him. He did it by taking away my other options."

"Are you okay, Velvet?"

"I will be. At least now I know the truth."

"You take care of yourself, Velvet. I hope you find a way to get away from him for good."

***

Velvet stormed into the front door of the shop just after opening time.

"You're late," Vano said, glancing up from some papers he was going through at the counter.

"And you're an asshole!" she snapped back, so furious she felt like smashing something.

He cocked a brow at her, his expression turning ice cold. "Excuse me?"

"You heard me."

There was dead silence in the shop as both Cooter and Finn stopped what they were doing and watched, their eyes shifting from one to the other.

Velvet glared at them. "You want popcorn with this show?"

"Don't be a bitch, Velvet," Vano said. "If you want to throw a tirade, let's go to my office." He grabbed her by the upper arm and yanked her ahead of him.

She jerked her arm free. "Don't fucking touch me!" She stomped down the hall and into his office.

He slammed the door and stuck a finger in her face. "Don't ever do that again, you understand me?"

She smacked his hand away. "No, you understand me. I know what you did, you son-of-a-bitch!"

He moved around behind his desk; she supposed he thought it was safer to put space between them, like she was some kind of hysterical woman. "What's the bug up your ass?"

"I had a nice little conversation with Aaron. He told me you and your thugs took the money that belonged to me."

"Velvet, don't overreact."

"Overreact? It was fifteen thousand dollars, Vano! It was my money! Not yours! You had no right to take it."

He leaned his fists on the desk. "I had every right to take it! I'm the head of this family. I decide how the money is spent."

She couldn't believe his logic, but then she really should because she knew he'd had that crap drilled into his head since he was young. He was twisting it all to serve his purpose, though. "You owed a debt, and you used *my* money"—she slammed her chest with her palm—"to pay it off. *Mine!* That money belonged to me! I didn't owe that debt, you did, Vano! I want my money back."

"Well, I don't have it anymore. So, you'll just have to wait."

"Wait? Wait for what?"

"I've got a deal going through. I'll make quite a haul. I can pay you then."

"No, Vano. I want it now."

"You'll get it when I give it to you, and you're not going to say another fucking word about it. And do you know why? Because if you do, I'll tell your precious boyfriend the truth. You think he'll stick around if he knows you're just a little street-rat con artist who's in town to take him and his brothers for another load of cash?"

"That's not true."

"Isn't it? Depends how you look at it. I bet I could put a spin on it that would have him believing you've been setting him up since the moment you hit town."

"You wouldn't do that; it would expose you, too."

"Think I give a shit what he thinks about me? But you, on the other hand, you my dear sister care about what he thinks of you, don't you?"

"I'm not going to live a lie, Vano. I won't."

"You'll do whatever I tell you to do and shut the hell up about it."

Velvet stared at her brother, and she knew what she had to do. She had to tell Liam, because she didn't want to be a part of any of this any longer. She didn't want to be a part of Vano's crimes. It was all so wrong. She'd have to take her chances with Liam and hope he'd believe her explanation.

Vano was running a horrible con; one she wanted no part of.

She thought about going to the police, but she couldn't bring herself to turn him in. It was ingrained in her—you don't turn on family. That was the gypsy code. But whether she gave him up or not, she knew she couldn't have anything more to do with it, and she wouldn't allow Vano to hold telling Liam over her head to keep her in line. The only thing she could do was to tell Liam herself before Vano did. Besides, she knew she couldn't keep her past a secret. She couldn't keep hiding it forever, not if her and Liam's relationship was real and not if she wanted a future with him.

CHAPTER SEVENTEEN

The photo shoot was scheduled for the next night.

Velvet arrived as soon as she could get away from House of Ink. She didn't want Vano to know what she was doing or where she was going. It didn't give her much time to spare before she was supposed to be ready. She'd brought some outfits, not knowing if they would have a stylist with wardrobe changes.

When she arrived, she saw it was truly a professionally run job, with a hairstylist, makeup artist, and even a lighting crew.

Liam hugged her. "You're just in time. I was going to call if you weren't here soon."

"I'm sorry. I got away as soon as I could."

He took her hands in his, threading their fingers together. "That's okay. You're here now."

"Liam, could I talk to you?" She looked up imploringly. She'd decided she couldn't go another day without confessing the truth to him. She should have told him days ago. Hell, she should have told him weeks ago.

He dipped his head. "Sure, baby. What's up?"

She glanced around the lobby where they were setting up the lighting. "Um, maybe in the break room or somewhere more private?"

A blonde woman approached. "I need to do your makeup and hair now, sweetie."

"Go with her. We'll talk after the shoot, I promise." Liam kissed her forehead, and the woman guided her to a chair in front of the mirror. Hair and makeup were a blur; all she could think about was how Liam would take the news she planned to drop on him later tonight. She closed her eyes. She had to put it out of her mind if she was going to do this shoot with all the professionalism it deserved.

Before she knew it, they were being called to the shoot. They'd dressed her in a skimpy bikini, and Liam was shirtless. The blinds were drawn and black paper was put up over the glass front door so that the shoot taking place in the lobby would be private.

The photographer motioned to her. "Over here on this leather couch would be great."

Velvet walked to the couch against the brick wall. Above it were several framed covers of Inked Up magazine - issues with Jameson on the cover. There were also beautiful examples of their work.

Liam sat down, his legs spread.

"Velvet, could you please sit on his lap, facing him, but look back at the camera." She got into position, and the photographer clicked off shots, pausing occasionally to adjust the lighting. "That's great."

Liam had his hands on her back.

"Okay, now move around the couch and get behind him." She climbed up and spread her legs over his shoulders, then leaned down to run her hands down his chest. They gave the photographer a lot of great shots. It was hard not to get caught up in the moment with Liam. All he had to do was look at her, and desire ran through her veins. The passion sparking between them, the heat, the intensity of emotion, none of these were put on for the camera. They were real.

"Now get back on his lap and face him again." She did. "Velvet, can we lose the bikini top? Show off your back?"

She looked at Liam.

"I'll make sure they don't see a thing, baby, but it's up to you."

She reached back and gave the tie a yank, pulling it free and dropping it to the floor.

He put his hands under her arm pits, his fingers stretching over her shoulder blades and pulled her to him, tilting his head up to look at her as she dipped hers down to stare into his eyes. His biceps covered the side of her breasts as he pressed them skin-to-skin.

The camera clicked off shot after shot. "These are great."

Jameson and Ryan stood in the back, watching the shoot. Velvet was used to having people watch her do photo shoots, and it didn't bother her.

The photographer moved in close for a few shots, and then backed off. "Velvet, can you face the camera?"

Liam looked up at her. "I'll cover you."

As she turned, he wrapped his forearm across her breasts.

The photographer clicked off a dozen more shots. "Turn sideways on his lap."

She did, and he stepped up to raise her arm. "Put your arm up like that, there with your palm against the brick."

It was her left arm that he moved, and the position had the inner side of her bicep right in front of Liam's face. He was gazing up at her with such heat and desire in his eyes. Every touch of his hand on her body had passion flaring through her and she couldn't believe how lucky she was to have him in her life.

Then his eyes dropped to her arm and focused in on the tattoo he'd inked there so many years ago, the unmistakable free hand sketch of a bunch of wild flowers. She watched his brows drop and then his eyes flicked up to her. She dropped her arm.

"Velvet, sweetheart, can you put your arm back?" the clueless photographer asked, but she barely heard him. The blood rushed to her ears, as the fact that Liam remembered that ink hit her.

"Liam—"

He put his hands on her waist, gripping tightly, and then he shoved her off him onto the couch. He stared at her in horror.

"You?"

CHAPTER EIGHTEEN

Liam stared at Velvet in shock. The room had tilted, and suddenly he was transported back ten years to the day he tattooed a young fifteen-year-old girl with a fake ID…

He stood, cleaning his station up, smiling to himself at the thought of how happy his last client had been with the work he'd done. He tattooed a lot of people, and often the tattoos were unimaginative and repetitive, and he would almost tune out. But some days there would be that one special client who would be so affected by the art and so happy with the finished product that it would make all of the less than imaginative designs worth it.

That girl he'd just tattooed had been one of those special ones.

The bell over the door jingled, and he heard footsteps across the floor. An irate, belligerent woman began yelling.

"Where's the owner? Which one of you criminals tattooed my underage daughter? I'm going to sue, that's what I'm going to do. I'll see this place shut down, and I'll take every dime you've got!"

Liam walked to the counter, and his eyes landed on the girl. He couldn't believe it. She was his last customer. His head pulled back at the look on her face. Her mother had a hold of her arm and was dragging her to the counter. The girl looked at him, her face a mask of shame and guilt.

Jameson came to the front and heard the woman's claims. A tick began in his jaw as anger flared through him. He glanced at Liam, and his eyes said it all; he couldn't believe Liam had been this stupid.

Liam had never felt as big a fool as he did in that moment. He watched Jameson count money into the woman's greedy hand, paying her off to sign the consent form and go away.

Liam knew, standing at that counter, witnessing that scene, that he had let his brother down in a way that would affect the shop and their business for possibly years to come, and he'd never forget it.

Velvet's voice brought him back to the present.

"Liam, please, let me explain." She covered her

breasts with her hands.

"It was you that day. It was your mother who shook Jameson down for a grand, and you just stood there and let it happen."

"I couldn't stop her. I'm so sorry."

"You knew. All this time we've been seeing each other. Of course you knew. You're standing in our damn shop, and you never said a word. You never had the guts to come clean to me."

"Liam, I wanted to tell you. I tried to tell you."

"Not hard enough."

"Please, you have to believe me."

"I don't have to do shit." He stood, staring down at her.

The photographer, the hair and makeup artists, the lighting guy, the reporter, and Jameson all stood staring, listening to every word.

Jameson shouldered his way forward. "Liam, what are you talking about?"

"Remember about ten years back when you'd barely opened the shop, that woman shook you down for a thousand dollars because I'd tattooed her underage daughter? This is the girl."

Jameson frowned. "You're sure?"

"It's her. I recognize the ink I put on her that

day. I just saw it under her arm. I guess I hadn't noticed it before. That or she's managed to keep it hidden." He spun back on her. "I don't suppose you'd want me to know, would you?"

"Is that true? It was your mother who took me for a thousand bucks?" Jameson snapped.

"I couldn't stop her. You have to believe me. Please."

"And you're in town at House of Ink. Why? The truth this time," Liam insisted.

"My brother talked me into coming to help him."

Liam's brows shot up. "That piece of shit is your brother?"

She nodded.

Jameson glared at her. "He screws customers over on a regular basis. Must run in the family. Your mother, your brother, you… You're all a bunch of thieving cheats, ain't that right?"

"No, please, you have to listen to me."

"Liam, get her the hell out of here."

"No, Liam, please, please just listen to me."

"Just get out, Velvet."

Jameson's face turned stone cold. He looked over at Ryan and ran a frustrated hand through his hair. "Looks like this photo shoot is a bust, man."

"I was just fifteen. I'm sorry. Please, you have to understand—"

"I'm done with you. It's all been just another joke to you, hasn't it?"

"No. I swear."

"You're not who I thought you were." He grabbed up his shirt and tossed it at her. "Get out."

She grabbed his arm. "Liam."

"If you've lied about this, what else have you lied about, or would you lie about in the future?" He yanked his arm free. "I just can't…" He couldn't look at her.

"I had no choice, don't you see?"

He spun back. "I see a liar and a thief. How could I ever be with someone like that? Someone like *you?*" He pointed at the door. "Get out!"

CHAPTER NINETEEN

Out on the sidewalk, Velvet stood in shock. It took a moment for everything that just happened to sink in. Shame flooded her body, quickly replaced by overwhelming pain and loss. Her shoulders shook, and she covered her mouth to keep from crying out the silent sobs that rocked her body. Liam's flannel shirt that she'd quickly shrugged on did little to protect against the night's chilly air, and she clutched her arms tightly to her chest.

Everything Liam accused her of, she couldn't deny. Her brother *was* conning people, and she *had* known it. Most importantly, she hadn't been honest with him about who she was, and she should have, right from the start, when he first approached her that night in the bar of the Excelsior Hotel. Perhaps then she could have explained everything; perhaps he would have listened then. But not now; now he was completely closed to anything she had to say, and hadn't he warned her that day up in the mountains when he'd confessed how closed off he'd been to relationships for fear of getting hurt?

Perhaps, deep down, she'd known this day was always coming, but that didn't make the overwhelming aching loss any easier.

She heard the door behind her open, and she turned to see Ryan Kelly stepping out. He approached her and held her trench coat up.

"I brought your coat. You left it inside." He held it open, and she turned and slipped her arms into the sleeves as he pulled it up over her shoulders.

"Thank you," she murmured, quickly wiping the tears from her cheeks.

"You okay?"

She shook her head silently and managed to choke out a shaky response. "No."

He looked uncomfortable and jammed his hands in his pockets. "I'm sorry the shoot ended that way."

She huffed out a breath, her eyes on the starry night. "I'm the one who should apologize. I hope this hasn't been a waste of a trip for you."

Ryan moved to stand next to her, studying the night sky as well. "Not at all. We got some fantastic shots. You and Liam have amazing chemistry, and it comes across in the photographs. The fireworks after... Well that proves there are deep feelings between the two of you."

"There *were*."

He looked over at her. "I'm sure there still are."

She spun on him then, the thought suddenly crossing her mind that this man could exploit everything he'd just witnessed in the article he planned to write. "Please, Mr. Kelly, don't use that part about them tattooing me when I was a minor in your article. It would ruin their reputation."

He searched her eyes. "That was quite a revelation in there. And call me Ryan, please."

"Ryan, I'm begging you, please. I've been the cause of so much harm already. If that went public, I…" She extended her arm toward the shop and let it hang there in the air a moment before letting it drop to her side. "I'd never forgive myself."

"I get the feeling you have quite a story yourself to tell. All you've been through—"

She pounded her palm to her chest. "*I'm* not important. Don't you see? It's Liam I don't want to hurt… At least not any more than I've already hurt him. Please, you can't print it."

He looked non-committal, and her heart lurched. Oh God, he might actually put it in his article.

"I'll make you a deal. I won't include that part if you do something for me."

Her eyes narrowed, and her lip curled up. Fucking hell, the guy was going to want sex in exchange for keeping silent. He was just another slim ball. "And what would that be, Ryan?"

He chuckled and shook his head. "Not what you're thinking, I swear. I just want you to tell me your true life story… on the record, for an article—about you."

Her mouth fell open. "You want *my* story? Why?"

"Because it sounds fascinating. I think it would make an amazing article."

"No. I can't, I…" Her voice trailed off, and her stomach dropped at the very thought of putting her life out there for everyone to see.

"It's up to you. I certainly can't force you to tell it."

Her eyes shifted to him. Oh, but he'd certainly use the revelations exposed to him today as leverage to get it from her, wouldn't he? Hadn't she been used and exploited her whole life just so other people could make a buck? She huffed out a laugh. Why would she think any of that had changed now? Wasn't that the recurring story of her life?

But if she didn't go along with him, could she live with herself when the article was printed about

Brothers Ink and it destroyed everything they'd worked so hard to build? Could she do that to Liam?

She knew the answer to that.

Still it irked her that Ryan was using this to his advantage. She lifted her chin and stared him down. "You know. I've let a lot of people use me in my life. I'm afraid you're just another one, and I'm done with that."

"I'm not trying to use you, Velvet."

"Oh, really? And why would you be any different? Why would you want to tell my story?"

"Because I feel like it's probably a really good story. Much more interesting than just a pretty girl with a lot of tattoos."

She bit her lip, considering. "And if I give you my story, you'll leave it out about them tattooing me?"

"Absolutely. I have no interest in ruining these guys."

Her brow rose. "You'll tell my story the way I tell it? The truth, no embellishments or omissions?"

"Well, just one omission—the part about Brothers Ink."

"Let me think about it."

"Don't wait too long. The magazine has a deadline, and my flight out of town leaves at noon tomorrow." He turned and walked back into Brothers Ink.

Velvet's eyes followed him, peering inside as the door opened for any glimpse of Liam, but he was nowhere in sight.

She turned back and watched a motorcycle roar past and thought of her first ride with Liam. She knew she'd never have another one, and the tears welled up again at all she'd lost. His kindness, his humor, his caring sincerity… she'd lost all of it.

Finally she turned and headed home. Thankfully, Vano was not there.

She crawled into bed, rolled to her side, and broke into tears, sobbing uncontrollably into her pillow.

After an hour, she grabbed her phone from the nightstand and tried to call Liam, but he wouldn't pick up. She dropped the phone on the nightstand with a clatter.

She'd lost him for good, and she had no one to blame but herself. She knew it, but that didn't make the pain any easier to take. It tore through her soul. In a lifetime of pain and loss, this was the worst she'd ever experienced.

Tomorrow she knew she'd have to pull herself

together, pick up the pieces of her shredded life, and move on, but not tonight. Tonight she just wanted to let the pain and tears wash over her as she slipped into a deep dark pit.

CHAPTER TWENTY

Liam strode upstairs to Jameson's office. He plopped down on the leather couch against the wall, his elbows on his knees, and tore his hands through his hair. He couldn't believe this was happening. How had everything gone to shit in the span of a few minutes?

The photo shoot had been going so well; he could feel the chemistry between them radiating through the room. He knew the shots the photographer was getting were smoking hot. He didn't need the guy to confirm it, but he had, telling them over and over that the shots were going to be fantastic.

It had all been so good. Maybe that was the problem. Maybe it had all been too good, and everyone knew if something seemed too good to be true, it usually was. He shook his head. Hell, wasn't this exactly the reason he avoided relationships? When they went to hell, it tore his damn heart out.

He stood and paced, ending up at the sideboard where Jameson kept a bottle of fine Irish whiskey. He poured a double shot into a short glass and set the bottle down hard, rattling the other glasses. Downing half of it, he resumed pacing, anger exuding off him.

How could he have misjudged this relationship so badly? How could he have misjudged her so badly? Had he misread every sign?

She'd loved what he loved, she'd gotten his humor, and fuck, the sex was off the charts. Her smile, the light in her eyes, the warmth of her touch when she'd rub his arm or lean in to snuggle against him… Had it all been a lie?

How the hell had this happened? How had he found himself in this position? Had he been blind? He felt like such a fucking fool.

He gulped down the rest of the drink and smashed the glass against the wall.

"Whoa, whoa." Jameson came up the stairs.

Liam collapsed onto the couch, running his palms down his face. "Sorry, man. Is everyone gone?"

"Yeah." Jameson pulled a chair over and sat, hunched forward, his head near Liam's. "You okay?"

Liam looked over at him. "No. I'm not okay. How did this happen? How could I be so stupid?"

"Come on, man; you're not stupid. She lied to you."

"I fucking tattooed her ten years ago. How did I not recognize her?"

"That fifteen-year-old chick she was back then is a hell of a long way from the woman who shot those sexy poses with you tonight. Besides, she had shorter, lighter hair, not the long black hair she has now. And I don't remember her eyes being that fucking blue. I'd bet the shop she's wearing colored contacts."

"Why? Has this all been part of another big con?"

Jameson shook his head. "Fuck if I know, but if her brother is running House of Ink, I'm wondering what he's really up to, because that place can't be making much. And as greedy as his mother was, I doubt he's any different."

"What's Velvet's connection? You think she's after something?"

Jameson huffed out a laugh. "I think she was after you, brother, big time. That chick was into you."

Liam shook his head. "Had to be part of some act, some play; I just haven't figured it out yet."

"You believe her?"

"What? That part about her wanting to tell the truth from the beginning?"

"Yeah."

"Then why didn't she?" Liam asked.

"You're asking me to explain the female mind?"

"I really thought we had something. You know? After all this time I've spent avoiding anything serious, I really thought she was it for me."

Jameson patted his knee. "I'm sorry, Liam. I hate like hell to see some chick fuck you over like this. You deserve better. A lot better."

"All I can think about was the moment you handed her mother all that money. I let you down, and I felt like such a fool. And now, what do I do? I bring her around again."

"Let the past go. That's done."

"How can you say that? I remember how badly that hurt you. Hell, Brothers Ink almost went under."

"Liam, it's over. Now is what's important."

"And what comes now?"

"That's up to you, brother."

"I'm sorry about the photo shoot. What did Ryan say? Are they pulling the article?"

"Nah. He got a shit-ton of great shots. Don't worry

about it."

"What about what was revealed to him? I did tattoo an underage girl. That's fact, Jameson."

"He promised he wouldn't put it in the article."

"Can you trust him?"

"I guess we'll find out."

CHAPTER TWENTY-ONE

The alarm on Velvet's phone went off, rousing her just after sunrise. She rolled to her back, still in her clothes where she'd collapsed in anguish the night before. Although she wanted nothing more than to give into the tears again at the thought of losing Liam, she knew she had to put that aside and be strong. She had to pick herself up and move on. She couldn't allow herself to break down again.

She had a decision to make this morning.

She stared at the ceiling and debated what to do about Ryan Kelly and his offer. The last thing she wanted was to have her pitiful life story out there for the world to see. She was ashamed of so much of it, but she also didn't want the reputation of Brothers Ink to be tarnished because of her. She'd done enough damage to them in the past; she couldn't bear it if she was the cause of any more.

In that moment, she knew what she must do. She'd have to tell her story—her real story, all of it, every degrading piece. And as she reconciled herself to this fact, she realized that getting it all out there was exactly what she needed. Maybe once it was all exposed, she wouldn't live in shame anymore. Maybe she could purge it from her soul for good. Perhaps that would be the only way she could take back her life.

Velvet got up, took a shower, and got dressed. Then she dug out Ryan Kelly's business card.

***

Ryan called the airline and changed his flight out to the next day. The magazine would be pissed at the fee it was going to cost them, but if Velvet's story was as good as he suspected, it would all be worth it.

A tap on the door to his hotel room had him up and crossing the room. He opened the door to find Velvet, and a tightness in his chest eased. He wasn't sure she'd show. "Hello, Velvet."

"I'm here," she whispered. "Let's do this."

He grinned. "Come on in, please."

He indicated the table and chairs by the third floor window where his recorder was set up. He also had a pad and pen so he could jot down any thoughts or impressions he had as she told her story.

"Would you like a drink?" he asked. "I have soft drinks, coffee, water?"

"Water is fine."

He got a bottle out of the mini fridge, cracked the top, and passed it to her. Then he took a seat opposite her.

She took a sip and asked, "Where do you want to start?"

He gave her a soft smile and turned on the recorder. "How about at the beginning?"

The corner of her mouth lifted. "I suppose that's a good place." She cleared her throat and took a slow deep breath, preparing herself. Then she shocked the shit out of him with her next words. "I grew up in a family of gypsies."

His brows shot up. "Gypsies? Like, for real gypsies? I didn't think they still existed."

Her knee bounced a mile a minute. "They do. We traveled the country, never staying in any town for long, just long enough for my father to pull some cons, get some money, and we'd move on. My father died when I was fourteen. My brother was only a year older than me. He wasn't ready to take over as head of the family, so it was my mom running the show. She soon proved she knew how to run a con just as good or better than my father. She was a strong woman, and as a widow she honed the tight rein on my brother and me.

"You have to understand, I was raised that men run the family, and women keep the home and children. My mother was especially strict, and she was just biding her time until my brother came of age and took over. In the meantime, she had to take on all the responsibilities my father would have handled. One included seeing to my future. In typical gypsy fashion, she made arrangements for me to marry another gypsy boy from a family in South Carolina—a boy I'd never met. I'm sure she was getting some money out of the deal, some form of dowry. Anyway, we were in Indiana that summer. What she didn't know was that I'd already met another boy, and we thought we were in love. We were young and stupid, and he had an older brother who knew a place that would tattoo us even though we were too young. Mason got the money, and we went down. He had the guy tattoo our names on each other.

"When my mom found out, she was furious. It was the ultimate betrayal in her eyes. How was she going to marry me off to another boy with Mason's name tattooed on my skin? She dragged me down to the shop and threw a fit, screaming at the guy and causing a scene. She threatened him with everything under the sun including legal action. I don't know that she would ever have done anything, but the guy didn't know that. He finally offered her two hundred bucks to sign the waiver and go away. The moment he offered her money, I could see the light bulb go off above her head, and right there, in that moment, my mother's biggest con was born."

He frowned. "What do you mean?"

"She got me a fake ID and sent me into place after place to get tattoos. Then she would storm back in with me in tow and threaten to have the place closed down for tattooing a minor. They'd all cave and give her a payoff to sign the consent forms. We hit place after place across seven states before I finally escaped at eighteen."

"My God."

"All the tattoos were complete crap, because most of the places were either seedy or just starting up; those types of shops made the best marks for a con like this because they either didn't want trouble with the law, had violations in the past, or they had new fledging reputations at stake. And it wasn't just the bad ink; she always had me pick shitty designs. They had to be for the con to work. Gross things no mother would want on her daughter's skin so as to make her outrage that much more effective. After I escaped, I had them covered over, one by one. All but the one Liam had done. That was the only time I defied my mother and picked a design I wanted—something that meant something to me."

"And his you kept."

"Yes. He was kind to me." She shrugged. "It meant something, and the work was beautiful."

"And the tattoos you have now?"

"I began to offer myself as a tattoo model in exchange for getting the old ink covered. I only went to the best shops, the best artists I could find."

"But not Brothers Ink."

"No, not there, for obvious reasons."

"You and Liam had some off-the-charts chemistry happening in that photo shoot."

She looked out the window, giving no response.

"You're in love with him, aren't you?"

She rubbed her palms over her upper arms several times, then nodded and turned to him. "You know I've been used by people my whole life. Exploited and used. Please don't be another one of those people. Please don't put the only thing I have left in the magazine. I told you my story. Don't use my feelings for Liam as part of it."

Ryan reached across the table and took her hand in his, giving it a squeeze. "I know you don't know me, and you don't trust me, but I promise you, Velvet, I won't do that. Listening to your story, I'm touched and moved by what happened to you. I promise, you'll like the story I write."

She pulled her hand away and reached for her water bottle, unscrewing the cap. "I didn't want to tell this story for obvious reasons, but maybe I need to tell it. Maybe, somehow in telling it, I'll free myself from the past and the shame. But the main reason I'm doing this is that I don't want Brothers Ink to be damaged by exposing that they've inked underage minors in the past."

"You have my word." He studied her a long moment. "Velvet, your story is fascinating. Have you ever thought about writing a book about your life?"

She let out a huff of laughter. "It would be an interesting story, but I can't even read."

He frowned. "What do you mean?"

"I mean I'm illiterate. My father never let me attend school. I can sign my name, and I can count money. Those were the only skills my father ever thought were important for a woman. I wouldn't know the first thing about writing a book."

"I could be your ghost writer. You tell me the story, and I organize it and put it down on paper."

She stared at him.

"Think about it. If you like the article I write, we'll talk."

"Ryan, you want the truth?"

"Isn't that what I've been getting?"

"Yes. I meant about what you just suggested. To me it sounds like just another pipe dream. You seem to be a sweet guy, and I hope you aren't a liar. But to be honest, whether I can truly trust you remains to be seen."

"I understand, but I still hope you keep the suggestion in mind."

"Let's just see how the article comes out."

"All right." He slid a document across the table and held out a pen. "This is a contract giving the magazine the right to print your story in exchange for this." He handed her a check. She could read her name and the amount. It was written for one thousand dollars. She looked up from the check she held in her hands to him.

"It's as much as I can offer you. We do the book, it will be much, much more."

She glanced down at the contract and pen lying on top.

"I can read it to you if you want," he offered. "Or if you want a lawyer to look it over, you're certainly welcome to do that."

"Read it to me."

He did, slowly, going over each part. When he was finished, she picked up the pen and signed her name. He stood and shook her hand. "I'm glad I got to meet you, Ms. Jones. You're a remarkable woman."

"I don't feel very remarkable today."

"I hope the article, in some small way, will be the beginning of changing that. I wish you nothing but the best."

"Thank you."

Velvet walked out of the hotel and stood on the street. She looked down at the check in her hand and knew what she had to do.

CHAPTER TWENTY-TWO

Velvet stepped through the door to Brothers Ink. There was a woman behind the counter, one she hadn't met before, and a couple of customers waiting. She approached the counter, peering farther into the shop, but she didn't see Liam.

Maxwell, who was showing a customer a design, glanced up and froze. He excused himself and came to the counter. "Let me handle this one, Ava."

She nodded, a questioning look on her face as she glanced between the two of them.

Max put his palms on the counter, looked at Velvet, and announced in a low growl, "Liam's not here. He's taking a few days off."

"I didn't come in here to see Liam. I need to speak with Jameson."

The woman beside him spoke up. "Is this Velvet, the woman I've heard so much about?"

Max glanced over at the woman. "Yeah. This is

her."

The pretty blonde surprised Velvet by extending her hand. "I'm Jameson's wife, Ava. It's nice to finally meet you, Ms. Jones."

Confused, Velvet took her hand. "You know about me?"

She gave Max a stern look. "I've got this, Max. You shouldn't keep your client waiting."

Max's jaw hardened, but he pushed off the counter without another word.

Ava turned back with a smile. "Sorry about that. You know how brothers are. They're pretty protective of each other." She paused, and her eyes swept over Velvet. "So, you're the one."

"The one who caused all the trouble? Yes."

"No, the one who finally won that big bruiser's heart," Ava corrected.

Velvet's jaw pulled to the side. "I'm confused. You don't hate me like the rest of them?"

"No. At least not unless you give me a reason."

"You don't have a reason?"

"Come with me. Let's talk in the break room."

Velvet's eyes cut to Max. He was definitely keeping one eye on her. "Are you sure?"

"Pay him no attention. Come on."

Velvet followed Ava through the shop to a room in the back. Ava walked to the coffee maker on the counter and dug two mugs out of the cabinet above. She turned to Velvet. "How do you take it?"

"A little sugar."

Once she'd poured them each a cup, she carried them to a table and they both sat.

"I'm not going to judge you," Ava said. "I don't know what happened when you were fifteen, but if these boys had the things they'd done when they were that age held against them, not a one would be able to talk."

"I appreciate that. Thank you."

"I don't know anything about your childhood or how you were raised or what kind of family you come from. What I do know is that you made Liam feel something and dare to open up to you."

Velvet looked down and nodded.

"And that's something he's never done with anyone. You are the first, so there must be something special about you. So, I'm giving you the benefit of the doubt."

"I never meant to hurt him. I should have told him the truth from the very beginning."

"Yes, you should have."

"And now it's too late."

"It may be. I don't know, but I hate to think anything is beyond hope."

"I hurt him so badly. He was afraid to open up and take a shot with anyone for fear of being hurt. And that's exactly what I did. Now he won't even speak to me."

"I think both of you are miserable right now. Perhaps that's a good sign." Ava studied her quietly a moment. "Do you love him?"

Velvet nodded, her eyes flooding with tears. She tried to fan them. "I promised myself I was done with crying."

Ava chuckled. "Sweetie, we women are never done with crying. Not when it comes to men." She reached her hand out and touched her arm. "I heard he tattooed you."

"Yes. He's good at what he does, and he knows it, but not in a cocky way, in a confident way."

"Yes, that's true," Ava agreed.

"He can talk to me about things I know nothing of, but he does it in a way that doesn't make me feel stupid."

"Why would he want to make you feel stupid?"

She shrugged. "Most people aren't so kind. In my experience, at least."

Ava gave her a soft smile. "I'm so sorry he's being stubborn now."

"I know Liam doesn't want to see me. That wasn't why I came."

"You said you wanted to talk to Jameson."

"I can't make it right with Liam, but at least I can right the wrong done to Brothers Ink and give Jameson the money my mother conned him out of."

"I see."

"Do you think he'll talk to me?"

Ava stood. "Come with me."

Velvet followed her out of the break room and up an open staircase. Ava paused at the top and put her finger to her mouth, indicating Velvet stay quiet.

The upper floor was all one open plan office. There was a huge desk at the far end set in front of a large window that looked out over the street. Jameson was sitting in a chair, his back to them, facing the window and talking on the phone.

Ava motioned her forward and tiptoed toward him. Velvet stopped in front of the desk while Ava crept around, slid her arms around her husband's shoulders, and kissed his neck.

The chair rocked, and Velvet heard the man tell whoever was on the phone that he'd have to call them back. Then he yanked his wife around to land in his lap.

She squealed.

"Well, this is a nice surprise, baby girl." He nuzzled behind her ear, his hand moving over her hip making a beeline toward her breast.

Ava caught his wrist, halting his progress just in time. "Um, darling, there's someone here to see you."

"Let 'em wait. I'm suddenly really busy."

"Baby, she's standing right there."

The chair rocked as Jameson swung his head around, and Ava scrambled off his lap.

"What are you doing here?"

"Darling, be nice," Ava warned.

"Liam isn't here, and if you've come to plead your case with me—"

Velvet laid the check on his desk. "I just wanted to give you that. I wanted to try to make things right, you know, for the money my mother conned you out of."

Jameson glanced at Ava, and then picked up the check, scanning the front. "You're giving this to me?"

"Yes. I signed it over to you."

"And why is Inked Up magazine paying you a grand?"

"That's not important."

Jameson's brows rose. "Yeah, I think it is."

Velvet sucked her lips into her mouth. She was so hesitant to tell him this part, but knew he wouldn't let it go. "Ryan Kelly paid me for my story."

"Your story?" Jameson tossed the check on the desk. "And what story is that? How you walked in here an underage minor and got ink?"

She shook her head. "No. He swore that would never be revealed. That was part of the deal."

"Deal?"

"If I gave him my life story, he promised not to include it in the article about Brothers Ink."

Jameson's jaw tightened. "You just keep comin' back around like a bad penny, don't you?" He jerked his chin toward the check. "You think this makes everything okay?"

"I know it doesn't. Nothing can make it all okay, but I have to try to make things right, to make amends. Maybe that amount of money doesn't mean as much to you now as it did back when you were first starting out, but it's a lot of money to me, and I need for you to take it. For me, if not for you."

"Jameson—" Ava started, but Jameson raised his hand, stopping her.

"You're right. It was a lot of money back then. Damn near broke this place."

"I'm so sorry. Please—"

"All right! Fine. I'll take your money. We're square. Now we're done here."

Velvet looked from him to Ava, who stayed quiet, but did it with a sympathetic expression on her face. Velvet nodded and backed away from the desk. She wanted to run, to dash down the stairs and flee toward the front door, but she forced herself to hold her chin high and walk out with all the grace she could muster.

***

When she was gone, Jameson ran a hand over his jaw. "Nothin' worse than a liar. I hate what she did to Liam."

"I know you do."

He pulled Ava onto his lap again. "And I hate that she ruined the good mood I was in five minutes ago."

Ava ran her fingers through his hair, massaging his scalp. She had a way of being able to calm the beast in him. It was one of the many things he loved about her. "Umm. That feels good."

"She loves him, baby."

"I don't want to talk about her, Ava."

"Liam should give her a chance to explain."

"Liam should run his own life, and you and I should stay out of it."

"Jamie—"

"Ava, I mean it. Don't go getting involved."

She stopped massaging his head and lay her head on his shoulder, breathing out a sigh. "I hate when love doesn't work out."

He cupped her head and played with her curls. "And I hate that my brother is devastated."

"I know. That's why we should try to get them back together."

"No, it's not." He tilted her face up to his. "I mean it, Ava. Liam's a big boy. He'll get past this. He'll find someone else."

She shook her head. "I don't think he will. You didn't see him, Jamie."

He frowned. "And when did you see him?"

"I went over there before we opened up. There was a nearly empty bottle of Jack on the coffee table, and he looked like hell."

Jameson lifted his chin toward the stairs that Velvet had gone down. "And she did that to him, Ava. Why would you want him back with her?"

"Because they love each other."

He ran a frustrated hand through his hair. "They work it out, then fine, they work it out, and I'll accept that fact, but I'll be damned if I'm helping that along. No, ma'am."

"Jamie…"

"How about you stop concentrating on your brother-in-law and give your husband some attention?"

***

Velvet walked back to House of Ink. On the way, she made a decision. With things over between her and Liam, she no longer had a reason to remain in Grand Junction. Leaving would require money, and she'd just given most of everything she had to Jameson.

She would need more, and she knew exactly where she was going to get it. Vano owed her money, but she knew hell would freeze over before he ever gave it to her. He wouldn't want her to leave again, and he'd make sure she didn't have the means to go.

So, that left her one option. She'd take it, either from the register or from the safe.

The O'Rourke's obviously didn't want her in town

anymore, and she wanted to get away from Vano, his illegal activity, and his creepy cohorts. In actuality, Liam was the main reason she'd stayed as long as she had. She knew all the reasons for leaving made sense, but still, somehow it felt like she was running. And that was a feeling she absolutely hated. It seemed like her whole life, as far back as she could remember, her family had been running from town to town, keeping one step ahead of the law.

She wished she could put a stop to Vano's con game against the seniors. Turning him into the police crossed her mind, but her whole life she'd been brought up that gypsies didn't rat on each other, and they stayed away from the law.

She'd have to figure that part out when she was safely away from Vano. For now she needed to concentrate on getting the cash and leaving.

Vano had two guys working for him slinging ink; an old guy named Cooter, and a young punk named Finn. Neither of them were very good, but they had one quality Velvet was grateful for today. They minded their own business and left her alone.

When she walked in the shop, both had customers and barely gave her a look, except for

Cooter's offhanded remark.

"You're late, Vee."

"Sorry. Is Vano here?"

"He's in the back."

Velvet's eyes strayed toward the hallway. He must be in the office, down the hall past the supply closet, the piercing room, and the bathroom. She moved behind the front counter and over to the register. Glancing surreptitiously over her shoulder, she saw both men had returned to what they were doing, paying her no mind.

Music blasted from one of their stations and it covered the sound as she popped the register open. She frowned. They'd only been open maybe an hour, but the register was stuffed full of money—way more than they could have possibly taken in this morning, especially with only two artists. Was all of this flowing in from the cons Vano was running?

My God.

She thumbed through a stack of hundreds. There had to be over two thousand just in hundred dollar bills.

"What are you doing?"

She nearly jumped out of her skin, turning to see Vano standing behind her.

"You scared the crap out of me."

"What are you doing, Velvet?" He grabbed her arm, yanking her from the register.

"I was just going to break a five for the vending machine." She tugged on her arm, but his grip was tight and twisting. "Vano, stop. You're hurting me."

He backhanded her across the face. "You stealin' from me?" He shook her violently. "Huh? Huh?"

The tattoo machines cut off, and the men looked over.

Vano's eyes cut to them, and he released her with a shove.

She stumbled backward, her hand coming to her burning face. "I swear I wasn't stealing."

He shook a finger in her face. "You better not, either. I keep a close count."

"What's with all the money, Vano?" she snapped.

"None of your business." He slammed the drawer shut. "I need you to run down to the post office and bring the mail from the PO box." He held the key out to her. "And be quick about it. You hear me?"

"Do it yourself!"

He grabbed her arm again, yanked her close, and growled low in her face. "You want more of the same?"

Her eyes went past him to Cooter and Finn, who sat stock still, watching, but apparently unsure whether to intervene. In the end neither had the guts.

Vano twisted to look and snapped, "Get back to work! This doesn't concern you. This is family business."

The machines immediately clicked back on and the furtive glances of the wide-eyed teens in the chair watched them.

"When are you planning to pay me? You've obviously got the money."

"Go do the errand! I'll give you your pay when you get back."

Violet yanked her arm free, eager to leave the shop, even if it was to run his damn errand. She grabbed the key from him and fled. Out on the street, she touched her hand to her aching face once more, wondering if it would leave a mark. It just proved that she had to get out of town as soon as possible.

***

Vano stood at the register, his hands on the counter, watching Velvet leave. He'd lost his temper, and he hadn't meant to. When he'd seen her thumbing through the stacks of money, he'd panicked. One of Skin's dealers had dropped it off, and he hadn't had time to take it to the safe, so he'd stuffed it in the register. Skin should know better than to have them dropping drug money off during business hours. What a bunch of idiots he was mixed up with.

"Problem?"

He spun to see Skin leaning against the wall of the hallway, his arms folded and a smirk on his face.

"No," Vano snapped. "Everything's fine."

Skin strolled up to Vano and got right in his face. He towered over him by at least four inches. He growled softly so the others couldn't hear, "She's been snooping around. You better pray she doesn't find out what the fuck her dear old brother's been up to. It'd be trouble for all of us. And you go treatin' her like that, she's gonna want to take off. Besides, I told you already, she's gonna be mine. What's mine, no one touches."

"She's not going anywhere. She's going to keep doing the deposits, and you're going to keep your mouth shut, and everybody stays happy and healthy."

Leaning down, Skin hissed, "You better pray that's what happens. 'Cause she causes us trouble, I don't care how hot she is, I'll get rid of her permanently. We understand each other? You clear on that?"

"Crystal."

Skin jerked his chin to the back. "Got another kilo to cut up. I'll be back tonight after closing."

Vano watched him saunter to the backdoor, wishing again he'd never hooked up with these assholes in prison.

CHAPTER TWENTY-THREE

Velvet walked the four blocks from the shop to the Post Office. Cool air hit her as she opened the glass door. A few people stood at the service counter to the right as she turned down the hallway where rows and rows of metal PO boxes lined the wall. There were so many, they went down and around the corner. She took out the key Vano had given her and searched for box 1492. It was the second row from the bottom down at the end. She cursed as she squatted down to open it, mumbling, "You couldn't get a box on the top row, could you, Vano? No, that would be too convenient."

Inserting the key, she opened the door and grabbed the stack of envelopes. When she did, she was shoved up against the wall from behind and her arm was twisted painfully behind her.

"You're under arrest for federal mail fraud," a deep male voice barked in her ear.

Out of the corner of her eye, several men in blue windbreakers materialized—from where she had no clue. She tried to twist around, but they kept her face smashed against the metal boxes as someone frisked her. She was sure she'd have an imprint of box 1488 pressed into her cheek. They didn't let her move until they had her hands cuffed. Then someone quickly read her the Miranda warning. She was pulled around and found herself face to face with a good-looking man in his thirties, dressed in a dark suit and tie. He was clean cut and had a swarthy Mediterranean look about him, but what stood out most was the FBI badge he flashed in front of her face.

"Bag up the mail," he ordered one of the other agents standing around her, all in blue windbreakers with FBI in large yellow lettering. Two of them grabbed her upper arms and hustled her down a back hall.

They moved out a rear entrance to several waiting black SUVs. She was put in the back seat of one. The man in the suit climbed in the front seat with the driver while two of the men in windbreakers climbed in on either side of her.

They didn't take her to the police station as she'd expected. They drove her just down the street to the Federal Building. She was brought in a side entrance and taken up an elevator to the third floor. When the doors opened, her eyes landed on the big FBI seal on the wall. It was intimidating as hell, and she was scared to death.

They manhandled her down a hallway, through a large office and into a small room with a table, two chairs, and no window.

One agent un-cuffed her hands from behind her back and cuffed one wrist to the metal arm on the chair while the other stood guard in the doorway. When she was secured, they left without a word.

"Don't I get a phone call?" Velvet called out as the door closed. She glanced around. There was a camera up in the corner aimed at her. She couldn't help sticking her tongue out at it.

She sat there, fear coiling in her stomach, and she thought she was going to be sick.

She didn't even have money for an attorney. Would Vano get her out of this? Who else could she call?

She was left alone for a good long time, long enough for her mind to go over every stupid decision she'd made that had put her here. She should have left town when Ryan Kelly handed her that check. She should have told Liam everything right from the beginning. She should have never agreed to come to Grand Junction with Vano in the first place. Hell, she should have never met him for breakfast that day in LA.

She huffed out a laugh and shook her head. It wouldn't have mattered. He'd already gotten to Aaron and taken all her money. At that point, there was no way he was leaving LA without her. He'd already set his plan in motion to get her back in the family fold.

She'd been so stupid.

The door opened, and the FBI agent in the dark suit walked in with a file folder tucked under his arm. He set a Styrofoam cup of coffee in front of her along with a handful of little packets of cream and sugar and a stir straw.

"I'm Special Agent Sanders." He sat in the chair across from her, tossed the folder down, and nodded to the steaming cup. "I didn't know how you took it."

"Thank you," she said, reaching for it eagerly.

"I can be civil. This doesn't have to be unpleasant for you."

Her brows rose. "I'm cuffed to a chair and charged with… What was it you called it? Federal mail fraud? It's a lot *unpleasant.*"

He fought a smile. "It's not you we want, Ms. Jones. I know you're just a pawn in this game. We want the mastermind behind this little con."

Velvet took a slow sip of her coffee. The gypsy code ran deep inside her, ingrained since she was old enough to understand. You never gave up family, and you never talked to the police. She wondered just how much Sanders knew. Was he already aware of Vano? Did he know he was her brother?

When she remained silent, sipping her coffee, her eyes darting across the fake wood grain of the table as she tried to out-think this man, he leaned forward, elbows on the table, not giving her time.

"Look, this can go one of two ways for you. You tell us everything you know and help us nail the people we're really after, and we work a deal where you do no jail time, or you continue the silent treatment and we book you."

When she still stayed quiet, he studied her long and hard until she began to squirm.

"Ms. Jones, do you know the penalty for Federal Mail Fraud?"

She shook her head.

"Twenty years in prison. For each offense."

Her eyes slid closed. *Oh my God.*

"That's a long time to spend in a cell."

"I'm innocent."

"You were the one with the key to the PO box—a box we know at least a dozen people mailed payments to, and that's only the ones who weren't too ashamed to admit they'd been conned. You think, if this goes public, victims won't be coming out of the woodwork?"

She thought about the phone calls she'd overheard at the shop. Those men had bragged about the amount of people they were conning and how easy it was. Agent Sanders was right; there would be hundreds more.

"Ms. Jones, my advice to you is to be concerned only about yourself. All the victims say it was a man on the phone, not a woman. Whoever you're protecting is not worth doing hard time in prison for. I'm prepared to offer you immunity if you cooperate."

"Immunity? From all charges?"

"Yes, if you help us catch the perpetrators. But you'll have to tell us everything you know, and you'll have to work with us to obtain evidence."

She dropped her head. She did not want to go to prison, not for something she didn't do. Was she as guilty because she'd known and hadn't reported it?

Maybe, but perhaps this was a way for her to do the right thing.

"Ms. Jones?" he pressed.

She blew out a slow breath. "My brother is involved."

Agent Sanders visibly relaxed.

She pinned him with her eyes. "I want it in writing—your deal."

He nodded and opened the file folder. He slid it across to her, pulled a pen from inside his jacket and held it out. "Read it. It's all there."

She looked from the document to him. "I can't."

He huffed out a breath. "So you're not going to cooperate? You'd rather rot in prison? Fine." He started to shove his chair back.

"Wait. I meant I can't read it."

He frowned. "Why not? You wear glasses or something?"

"No. I *can't read!"* she snapped, all the tension of the moment getting to her. A tear slid down her cheek. As much trouble as she was in, she was still almost as ashamed to admit that fact as she was to be involved in all this.

Agent Sanders ran a hand over his jaw. "I'm

sorry. I had no idea. Shit." His eyes shifted to the side and he tapped the pen on the desk. "Okay, look, I can get the DA in here to explain it to you, or I can let you call your lawyer."

"DA?"

"District Attorney."

"Oh."

"If you call a lawyer… Well, once they're involved, these deals always go sideways." He tapped his finger on the paperwork. "This is a fair deal, Ms. Jones. You cooperate, you go scot-free. We almost never make deals like this. I'm talking no jail time, no probation, and no record of any kind. That's unheard of. I went to bat for you, because I've been watching you and—"

"Watching me?"

"We've had the shop under surveillance for weeks now."

So they already knew everything? "Then why don't you arrest Vano and his creepy friends?"

"Because I need solid evidence to nail them, and you're going to get it for me."

"Me?"

"You're the only one who can. And you're going to do it, because you're a good person. Do you know they took money from the elderly? Almost all of them on social security, barely making ends meet. These guys have no morals, no scruples, but you do, don't you, Ms. Jones? I've investigated your background. You've, for the most part, had nothing to do with your family since you became an adult. You've got no criminal record, hell not even a parking ticket. Why would you take the fall for this? You shouldn't have to, not when you can help me put the ones responsible behind bars. And that's what you're going to do, aren't you?"

She looked down, letting out a deep surrendering sigh, but still the words stuck in her throat. Could she actually do it?

"You know, Ms. Jones, I know about your gypsy family."

She snapped her head up.

"I know about the years your brother did in prison. I know your father was wanted in four states before he died. I know your mother wrote bad checks in multiple states." He studied her a moment. "You were brought up in that family. You weren't given a choice. Your brother's been running cons with your father since you were in grade school."

"I was never in grade school."

He took in a slow breath. "I suppose you weren't. I know how gypsy families are. I know it's the men who run things. I know you probably didn't have much to do with any of this. The bruise on the side of your face proves that. Your father died when you were young, and your brother's been running the show since the day he turned eighteen. Yes, I know your story, Veleena."

At the use of her real name, her eyes narrowed. She supposed it shouldn't surprise her; he'd thoroughly checked her out.

"You've had no one to save you since you were a child, you've had to save yourself. Well, now you're going to save yourself again, Ms. Jones. And I don't want you to feel one moment of guilt for doing it."

He was right. It was up to her. "All right. Tell me what I have to do."

He smiled. "You're making the right decision."

"I hope so."

"I'm going to release you. We've made copies of all of the mail in the box, recorded the serial numbers of the bills. I'm giving it back to you, and you're going to take it to the shop just like normal. We're going to be watching for it to pop up in the next bank deposit, which I'm assuming will be dropped off as usual by you."

He knew it all. Obviously he hadn't lied about having the shop and her under surveillance.

"I'm going to give you some tiny cameras and audio surveillance equipment to plant around the shop. You need to get me something, some kind of useful information or evidence. Understand?"

She nodded. "Yes, sir."

"I'll give you forty-eight hours to bring me something. Meet me at the Sunrise Diner at 3:00 PM day after tomorrow."

"What if I can't get anything?"

"You will. I have faith in you, Ms. Jones."

Velvet never thought she'd be responsible for sending her brother back to prison, but it looked like she was going to have to do it. What choice did she have?

"One more thing. You try to leave town, I'll know."

She supposed that meant they'd have eyes on her. Normally, that would make her uncomfortable, but considering how dangerous Vano and his accomplices could be, maybe having agents watching her was a good thing.

CHAPTER TWENTY-FOUR

Liam sat in his truck, slumped down in his seat, a hat shading his eyes from the sunrise when Pam pulled into the shelter's parking lot. He heard the engine cut off and her car door open and shut, and still he didn't move.

Her knuckles rapped on his window. Finally, he straightened, dragged the hat from his face, and rolled down the window.

"You look like hell," she stated.

"Good morning to you, too."

"You're here early. What time did you roll out of bed?"

"Who says I've been to bed?"

Her chin lifted, and she frowned. "Since when are you the type to stay out all night? You been drinking?"

"Not in hours. I'm sober."

"Um hmm. Come on in. I'll make coffee."

She was such a mother hen, but right now, that

was what he needed. He knew he could go out to the farm and get the same thing from Ava or Mrs. Larsen even, and he probably would eventually, but right now he needed to let what happened with Velvet filter through someone who had more distance, someone who he knew would tell him straight and not just take his side. He needed to know if he was wrong.

The truck creaked and rocked as he climbed out and slammed the door.

The keys jingled as Pam unlocked the glass door and let them both in, locking up behind them. The place wouldn't open for almost an hour.

She dumped her purse on the counter, and Liam trailed her down the hall to the small break room. She grabbed the glass carafe from the coffee maker and stepped to the sink.

Liam leaned his hip against the edge of the counter and crossed his arms, watching the water slowly fill the pot.

"So? Spill. What's going on with you?"

His bloodshot, tired eyes met hers, and he sucked in a deep slow breath, then shook his head and looked away. "Everything's gone to shit. I don't even know where to start."

"What do you mean everything?"

"I met this girl."

"Ah, a girl. That's the best kind of trouble."

He gave a short huff of breath. "Not this one."

Pam moved to the coffee maker and filled the tank, then shoved a filter in the basket and spooned in grounds. The aroma carried to Liam, and he breathed deep, hoping it would wake him up.

She finished and flipped the "on" switch. "Sit. Let's talk."

He pushed off the counter and dragged a chair out from the table. It gave an awful sound as it skittered across the linoleum. Nails on a chalkboard—that's what flashed through his tired brain. He sat heavily.

Pam took the seat beside him. "Have I met this woman?"

He shook his head. "No, but I've been seeing her a while."

"Where did you meet?"

"A tattoo expo in LA."

Pam frowned. "A long-distance romance?"

"Nope. She moved to town."

"Really? So what's the problem?"

"She's not who I thought she was. I found out she lied to me about her past."

"Anything you want to share?"

He shook his head again. "She tried to explain; I didn't really give her the chance, but it's big. I'm not sure if it would matter—the why of it, I mean. It happened."

"I'm getting the feeling this thing that happened, happened to you?"

"Yeah, well, to the shop. Her family scammed Jameson out of a lot of money, partly because I was an idiot and did something stupid. It's a long story."

"So, you cut her loose, I take it?"

"Yeah."

"And now you regret it? Is that what's bothering you?"

"I guess. I mean… Hell, I don't know what I mean. I just feel like I was really quick to judge her and end it. It was the shock of it, the fact she lied, the heat of the moment. Now—"

"Now you want to take it all back?"

He ran a hand down the back of his neck. "Not take it all back, but… Maybe I just need to know what she was doing with me, ya know? Was it all some plan to… I don't know what."

"She's the one who initiated the relationship?"

"That's the thing. That's what doesn't make sense. I

was the one who pursued her, not the other way around."

Pam stood and poured the coffee, carrying them to the table and setting a steaming mug before him. His palms wrapped around it, taking in the warmth as he stared into the black liquid.

She sat again. "What you need Liam, is closure. And from the looks of those bags under your eyes, you're not going to rest easy until you get it."

At the reminder of how tired he was, he brought the mug to his mouth and took a big gulp. "Everyone tells me I should just stay away from her, just leave it alone and move on."

"I see."

His eyes darted up to hers, wondering if she agreed with them, almost willing her to deny it, but afraid she wouldn't.

"Obviously, that's not working for you."

He let out a breath and felt a million tight muscles relax. "So, I should talk to her?"

She gave him an indulgent smile. "Honey, you knew the answer to that before you walked in here. But I'll spell it out for you, because I think you need it right now. Yes, that's what you should do, Liam. Communication is always the key to a relationship.

And ending it like that, without talking it through? It's not fair to either party."

He nodded. "Thanks."

"Can I give you a little advice about women?"

The corner of his mouth pulled up. "I suppose I need it, huh?"

"Never met a man who didn't." She grinned back, then leaned her elbows on the table, dipping her head close. "Listen to her. Listen, listen, and then listen some more, then speak."

He nodded. "I'll try."

"Lying destroys trust; I'm not going to say it doesn't, but we all lie at some point. Sometimes to avoid hurting someone we care about, or we don't want them to think badly about us, or to protect our own selfish interests. She may have been worried she'd lose you. In any case, it was wrong because her lying took away your right to decide whether her behavior was acceptable or not.

"Look, bottom line, I can't tell you what to feel or what to do, but the past is best left exactly there—in the past. If she hasn't done anything to wrong you in the present, only you can decide if you want to try and make a go of it. Look at it this way, you've already been hurt, so what's the worst that can happen?"

"I suppose."

"Be honest about what you want from the relationship—with yourself and her. If you're going to end it, do it by treating her with dignity, even if you think she hasn't deserved it."

He nodded again. "Thanks for the talk."

She touched his forearm. "You're like a son to me, Liam. I want you to be happy. If she's the one, you better bring her to meet me."

He leaned over, kissed her forehead, and teased, "Thanks, Ma."

She rolled her eyes. "Go clean the cages."

CHAPTER TWENTY-FIVE

Velvet stood at the counter, her eyes shifting to the clock on the wall. It was almost closing time, and the last customer's ink was about finished. Finn was cleaning off the man's skin. Cooter was cleaning up his station.

Velvet drifted quietly down the hall to the break room. She took a moment to glance around the room, wondering where to hide the dice-sized cameras that Sanders had given her. The sink and counter had been disgusting when she'd started working here, and since then she was the only one who'd cleaned it. She decided to stash it between two spray bottles of kitchen cleanser, a place she knew the men would never bother with. She aimed the device at the table and chairs, then went over and stuck the tiny audio transmitter under the tabletop.

She spun, checking over her shoulder, but there was no one there. She was glad to be able to get the two devices planted easily enough. Now she just had one more place to bug: Vano's office. That part was going to be tricky; he always kept his office locked and never let her in there alone. She bit her lip, knowing she'd have to think of a way to accomplish the job.

She returned to the front. Finn brought his client to the register to ring him up, and Velvet straightened aftercare product on the shelves, keeping an eye on what Finn was doing. Her mind raced, trying to come up with a plan.

Finn finished up and walked the client to the door, then flipped the lock. "Time to crank the tunes!" he hollered out. "You got any beer in the fridge, Cooter?"

"Yeah, should be some. Get me one, will ya?"

As Finn moved toward the back, Velvet ran an end-of-day report on the register and counted out the till. Glancing surreptitiously over her shoulder to make sure Cooter wasn't watching, she quickly snapped a picture with her phone of the total amounts on the register tape.

Finn returned with three bottles of beer and set one on the counter for her as she slipped the phone into her pocket. "Have a cold one, Velvet?"

"Thanks, Finn."

He gave her a wink and walked back to his station,

pausing along the way to crank up the stereo. Pulsing rap music filled the place, bouncing off the walls and vibrating the glass in the door. Velvet tried to concentrate on counting, but the noise made her lose track several times.

Vano walked up behind her, startling her, then yelling over at Finn, "Turn that shit down and hit the road."

Neither Finn nor Cooter argued with Vano. Finn grumbled a little, but got up to do as he'd been told.

"I'll do this." Vano slipped the bills from her hand and took over the counting. The worn faded money slid easily through his hands, bill after bill, *shup, shup, shup*; the stack of increasing denominations was quickly tallied up. He glanced over at her as he stuck the money in a zipper bag. "You want to take this to the bank and put it in the drop box tonight or take it in the morning?"

Velvet hated taking that much money at night, even with the FBI watching her every move. She knew saying no would also make him take it to the safe. Maybe that would be her chance. Plus then she'd get to take it into the lobby in the morning and give it to the teller where she could verify the amount being deposited. She could snap a picture of the receipt to compare with the total from the register report and give the information to Sanders. She had no doubt they wouldn't match up. "I'll take it tomorrow."

Vano headed to his office to put the bag in the safe, and she tagged along behind him. She dug one of the audio devices out of the hip pocket of her jeans and closed her palm tight around it. "Can I talk to you, Vano?"

He stopped in the hallway, turning to her. "Yeah? What?"

This wouldn't do; she had to get him in the office. She nodded to the door. "It's kind of private."

"Fine," he snapped and led her inside the room. She sat in the chair in front of his desk as he closed the door and moved behind the desk, squatting down in front of the safe. Quickly, she pressed the magnetic device to the underside of his old metal desk.

He finished, locked the safe, and stood, turning back to her. "So, what did you want to talk about?"

"Um, well, you know I haven't asked about mom in a while, and I was just wondering how she was doing?"

Vano sat, a doubting expression on his face. "Now, all of a sudden you care? She's been in that nursing home six months."

Velvet tried to fake concern for a woman who'd mistreated her for her whole life, but she didn't want Vano to become suspicious, so she did her best. "We never got along, it's true, but she's still my mother." She shrugged. "I just wondered how she was."

"She's fine, as well as can be expected. She barely remembers who I am anymore. You should go visit her while she's still got any cognitive skills left."

Velvet looked away. She'd hated her mother for so long. Could she actually see her mother now and feel any differently? Could she ever forgive her? Would that forgiveness help Velvet to finally let go of the past and truly put it all behind her? Hanging onto the bitterness certainly wasn't hurting her mother any longer; the woman probably didn't even know who she was. No, hanging onto all that baggage was only hurting herself now.

Perhaps when everything was over and Velvet got herself out of this mess, she'd go see her mother. After all, if things went the way Agent Sanders wanted, Vano wouldn't be visiting her anytime soon. Her gaze flicked to him. "I suppose I should. Maybe I will. I'll…I'll think about it. The place… Is it nice?"

"As nice as those places can be."

"You can afford that?"

"I manage. I prepaid for the year. They gave me a discount."

She nodded. "I see. So she's paid up till the end of the year then."

"Yep. Although the doctors think the disease is progressing rapidly. She may be in a vegetative state before then."

"Oh. It's that bad?"

"Yep." He leaned back in his chair, his hand rubbing his mouth, studying her. "I know she wasn't a good mother to you, especially after Pop died, but she didn't have an easy life either, Vee. She had to marry a man she didn't love, and he was a jerk to her. You may have been daddy's girl, but—"

She stood abruptly, having no interest in rehashing her childhood. "Fine. I said I'd think about it." She turned to leave.

"Vee."

She paused at the door. "Yes?"

"I hated it."

"Hated what?"

"What she did to you."

"But you didn't stop it, did you?"

He had no comeback for that. His eyes dropped to her jaw, and he jerked his chin at it. "I'm sorry about that. I didn't mean it."

She shook her head. "You never do, Vano. You're more like Mom than you know. You always have been."

For that he had no reply.

She turned and left. Her hand was shaking as she pulled the door shut behind her and leaned against the wall. She wished for the hundredth time she'd never come here. Except then she wouldn't have had all the time she'd had with Liam. She wouldn't trade that for anything, but it was over now. The pain of losing him descended over her again, and she closed her eyes. She couldn't think about that now. She had to get herself out of the mess she was in, and no one could help her, no one could save her. Like Sanders had told her, she had to save herself.

She hadn't been able to plant the tiny camera in Vano's office, but at least Agent Sanders would be able to hear everything he said in there, every meeting with Thing One and Thing Two as she'd come to think of Skin and his buddy.

Which reminded her, she needed to get the hell out of here. She didn't want to be around when those two showed up, and they always showed up not long after closing time. Grabbing her purse, she headed out the back door.

CHAPTER TWENTY-SIX

"Has Liam come in yet?" Jameson tapped a pen on his desk, his eyes connecting with Max slumped casually in the chair in front of him.

"Not yet."

"Have you talked to him?"

Max shook his head, crossed his leg, and put his boot on his opposite knee. "I've tried, but he's kind of closed down. If I bring it up, he changes the subject."

Jameson's eyes dropped to his desktop. "I guess we just need to give him time. He'll come out of it eventually."

Both men looked toward the stairs as the sound of someone running up them carried through the space.

Ava dashed in. "Jamie, you've got to see this."

He frowned. "What?"

She put a copy of Inked Up magazine on the desk before him. There was an amazing shot of

Liam and Velvet on the cover. On a small Post-it note attached was scrawled the note, *Hitting newsstands Friday--Ryan.*

"It just arrived by messenger," Ava murmured.

Maxwell whistled. "Wow. Great shot."

Jameson glanced up at Ava as he flipped the pages. "You read the article."

She nodded, but he caught a funny expression on her face. She looked kind of shell-shocked.

"What's wrong? Is it bad?"

She shook her head. "No. It was great. The shop is described as still the primo shop for color and shading. The pictures are gorgeous."

Max came around behind Jameson and bent over his shoulder. "The chemistry between them really comes across in those shots, doesn't it?"

Jameson skimmed the article, searching for any mention of Velvet. "Liam and Velvet are described as the 'it couple' in the world of ink right now."

"Did he put that other shit in the article?" Max asked.

Jameson shook his head. "I don't see it."

"It's not mentioned. I checked," Ava confirmed.

Jameson let out a sigh of relief. "Thank God."

"There's more."

Ava's quiet admission brought his eyes up. He frowned. "More?"

She reached down and flipped to another article.

He stared down at the two-page spread. On the left was a black and white, slightly out of focus shot of Velvet staring out a window. She looked vulnerable, her eyes glassy. The tagline below her picture read: *The tragic true story of the hottest tattoo model around.*

On top of the adjacent page in bold black typeface it read: *How America's hottest ink model resurrected her life from a heartbreaking childhood of abuse.*

Jameson read the story out loud.

We photographed the accompanying shot of Velvet in black and white because this story is not about the colorful ink on her skin, but about how she got it. Velvet is beautiful, but there is nothing beautiful about her story.

Born into the life of scammers and con artists with a family that was always on the move, always one step ahead of the law, young Velvet barely stood a chance.

The three of them bent over the story as Jameson read to the end. He lay the magazine down. "Jesus, I had no idea."

"That's fucked up, man."

Jameson met Ava's eyes, and she murmured, "Liam needs to see this. He needs to know the truth."

"Is he here yet?"

"He wasn't when I came up here. It was just Rory downstairs."

Jameson stared down at the magazine. "That woman was one money-hungry bitch. Who does that to their daughter?"

They heard Rory and Liam's voices in conversation downstairs arguing about a Broncos game.

Jameson looked at Max. "Go get him."

Max strolled to the staircase and hollered down. "Liam, got a second?"

His answer carried up the stairs. "I do not actually."

Max growled back, "Let me rephrase that. Get your ass up here!"

Jameson lifted his brow.

Max grinned and sat a hip on the edge of the desk as they waited.

The sound of Liam trudging up the stairs carried to them, and he came into view. He frowned when he saw all three of them around the desk. "What's up?"

"The new issue just came in." Jameson held up the magazine, and Liam's eyes dropped to the sexy shot of himself and Velvet on the cover. His face went ashen.

"Oh." He just stared at it.

"The article was great," Ava whispered.

He nodded, with barely any emotion showing on his face. "Good."

Ava took the magazine and opened to the article about Velvet. "You need to read this."

He glanced down at it, and his expression changed to one of stunned disbelief. "What the hell is that? She conned the reporter into doing an article on her?"

"Read it."

He shook his head. "No."

Ava started reading it aloud.

Liam jerked the magazine from her hands and slapped it on the desk. "I said I don't want to hear it!"

"You need to, brother," Jameson advised. "It's pretty shocking."

"Shocking? How?" When he wouldn't elaborate, Liam glared at him, but finally picked up the magazine and sat in a chair, reading it slowly.

"She was a victim, bro. Worse than this shop was. What was done to her was damn right child abuse."

When Liam finished, he tossed the magazine on the desk and buried his head in his hands. "Jesus Christ. I wouldn't even give her a chance to explain."

Ava squatted next to his chair and touched his forearm, gently pulling his hands from his face. "Liam, did you know she couldn't read?"

He pinned her with pain-filled eyes. "I had no clue. I would have helped her."

"You didn't know."

He bit his lip and shook his head. "I should have listened. I should have given her the benefit of the doubt."

Jameson hated to see him like this, and he didn't know if what he was about to confess would make it better or worse. "Brother, I need to tell you something."

Liam stared at him, waiting as if for the other ball to drop.

"She, uh…" Jameson dropped his eyes to the desk and slowly rubbed his hands together.

"Just say it."

"She was paid a thousand dollars for that story. She came to apologize, and she gave the check to me. Signed it over to pay back the money I gave her mother ten years ago."

He frowned. "When was this?"

"The day after the shoot."

His brows shot up. "And you're just telling me now?" He surged to his feet. "Goddamn it, Jameson."

"I'm sorry." His eyes cut to his wife's, then back again. "I should have told you that day, but I thought you were through with her, and hell, I didn't know about any of this." He nodded to the magazine.

Liam's gaze dropped to it. "I have to find her. I have to talk to her. Now. Today." He spun.

Jameson stared at his brother's retreating back as he moved to the stairs and dashed down them, then his gaze met Ava's. She grinned in that, *I was right,* way she had. He rolled his eyes, and she burst out laughing. Jameson glared at her. "Go ahead and say it."

She smiled huge and did exactly that. "Told you so!"

CHAPTER TWENTY-SEVEN

Velvet sat in a booth in the back of the diner, her nails clicking against the thick coffee mug. It was five minutes after three. Her eyes scanned the street outside for Agent Sanders. It was hard enough coming up with an excuse to get out of the shop, but she felt like a sitting duck. What if one of the guys ran out to grab a cold drink or food? Hell, they could walk right past here.

Being left waiting was fraying her nerves, and sneaking around had them already worn down. She wasn't sleeping, she was barely eating, and she was a nervous wreck most of the time.

The door opened and she glanced up. Sanders walked in and pulled his shades from his eyes. It only took him a second to spot her.

"Hello, Velvet," he said, sliding onto the red vinyl seat.

A waitress came over. "What can I get you, honey?"

"Coffee. Thanks." When she walked away, he glanced at Velvet. "You look tired."

"I'm not sleeping much."

The waitress returned with the carafe and a mug. "Did you want to order food?"

"No, thank you. Just this," Sanders replied. When she'd retreated, he snagged a couple packets of sweetener from the bowl, tore them open, and dumped them in his mug. He stirred it slowly, his eyes studying Velvet. "What do you have for me?"

Her hand slipped into the pocket of her jacket, and she pulled out her phone. She showed him the pictures she'd taken of the register receipt and the deposit slip. There was almost two thousand more in the deposit.

He took her phone and texted the photos to himself. "Good. If the serial numbers from the PO Box money show up, it will prove he's laundering money through the business in addition to mail fraud."

"So am I done?"

He shook his head. "We were able to pick up some conversations in his office. There are other business accounts. There's much more money going through that business than just the phone scam. We need to know where it's coming from. If they won't talk about it, we need you to see if you can find something."

"Can't you just break in after hours or something?"

"If we were discovered, we'd have to move too soon. I want this case locked down with air tight evidence."

"These men" —she fiddled with her fingernails—"are not nice men. They're dangerous."

"I understand."

"Do you?"

"Look, we overheard them talking about some shipment coming in tomorrow. They talk quietly, and we just can't pick it all up. We don't know what the product is. Could be counterfeit goods—"

She cut him off, dread filling her. "Or drugs."

He nodded. "Yes, if I had my guess, cocaine or heroin. But it could be anything. We need you to find out for us."

"They're already suspicious of me. They watch me like a hawk. I had to make up a story just to meet you. My brother thinks I'm out buying tampons."

"I'm sorry, but this is the deal we made. You cooperate—"

"I *am* cooperating!"

"*And* you help us get evidence."

"I'm living a lie, and I hate it."

"I know this is difficult for you, but that was the deal."

"Fine!" She started to slide from the booth, but his hand reached out and gripped her wrist.

"Same place, same time tomorrow."

She yanked her arm free. "Great. How many accidents do you think I can have?"

He grinned. "You'll think of something. If it's one thing I've discovered about you, *Veleena,* it's that you're a very resourceful woman."

"Fuck off, Sanders." She stormed through the diner and out the door. What a jerk, and now she'd been gone too long; Vano was sure to question her. Velvet strode down the street, but she couldn't get what Sanders had told her out of her head. This whole time, she'd thought this was a simple con her brother was running. But now the FBI thought her brother was involved in laundering drug money. Could it be true? Or was it even worse? Was he actually involved in dealing the drugs himself?

She'd bet her last dollar that whatever was going on, the show was being run by those two ex-cons he'd met in prison. Vano had seemed off lately, like he was under extreme pressure, and that just didn't make sense, especially with as much money as was rolling in. Those men had to have something they were holding over him, or maybe they were just threatening him. Vano was never one to be easily coerced to do anything, but in the end he was just a small time con artist. Those ex-cons were a whole different league of criminals.

And now Sanders wanted her to dig deeper into their activities. She could really put herself in danger.

Velvet walked around the corner, her head down, her eyes on the sidewalk. She tried to figure out what to do when she collided hard with the solid chest of a man. She stumbled back, and her mouth fell open. "Liam."

He was just as stunned to see her, but he recovered quicker. "Velvet. I was actually just heading across the street to your shop."

She frowned, her brain, like a car that missed a gear, was slow to make sense of his words. "House of Ink?" She swallowed. "Why?"

"I need to talk to you."

"About what?" She didn't want to let herself hope. This could be about anything. Maybe she'd left something at his apartment.

"I saw the article."

That was the last thing she expected him to say. She frowned. "The article?"

"The one you sold to Inked Up."

"Oh." God, with everything going on, she'd forgotten about it. It was hard to read his face. Was he pissed she'd sold her story, like Jameson had been? Maybe he'd been on his way to the shop to tell her off.

"You haven't seen it?" he asked, his brows dipping.

"No."

"Jameson got an advanced copy sent to him today by Ryan."

Velvet looked off down the street, her mind in a fog and murmured, "Maybe it's in the mailbox." Her eyes came back to his, and she frowned. "You read it?"

He nodded. "I had no idea you went through all that."

"What did it say? Did Ryan make me sound pathetic?"

"Not at all. The story was very well written, very respectful of you." He studied her. "Velvet, I…I can't believe you were put through all that. Why didn't you tell me?"

She huffed out a laugh. "Who would want to tell a

story like that one? I'll be a pathetic fool from coast to coast now."

He grabbed her arm and pulled her close. "Don't say that."

She pushed him back. "I have to go."

"Wait. Please? I'm sorry I didn't give you a chance to explain. I'm sorry about all of it. Can we go somewhere and talk?"

He sounded so sincere and sweet. She gazed off in the distance, and suddenly everything came crashing down on her. She felt her eyes sting and flood with tears, and she couldn't stop herself from breaking down in front of him. Her hand clasped tightly over her mouth to keep the sobs that shook her body from escaping.

He frowned down at her, completely stunned. "What is it?"

She shook her head and tried to push past him, but he grabbed her arm and pulled her back, then drew her into the alcove of a doorway.

He cupped her face. "Velvet, tell me what's wrong."

She stared up at him, her body trembling and finally confessed. "I'm in trouble, Liam."

"What kind of trouble?"

"The FBI is after Vano, and they're using me to get to him."

"What? How?"

"It's a long story."

"I've got all the time in the world, Velvet. Talk to me."

She shook her head. "I can't. I've been gone too long."

"Walk down the street with me. We'll get in my truck and drive somewhere. You're not going back to that damn shop. No way in hell."

"Liam, but…"

"Come on." He took her arm and led her quickly down a back street, over two blocks, and came up behind Brothers Ink. His truck was parked in the alley. He jerked the passenger door open. "Get in."

"Liam—"

"Get in."

She quickly scooted in, and he jogged around and got in the driver's seat.

"Where are we going?"

He twisted in the seat, his hand gripping her headrest, and stared intently into her eyes. "Do you trust me?"

She did, with all her heart. "Yes, but—"

"We're going to go somewhere and talk, somewhere away from here. And I promise you we're going to figure this all out together. Okay?"

Relief flooded through her body. Someone was going to help her; not just someone—Liam, the most important man in her life. "Okay. But where?"

"We once talked about camping, remember?" Liam looked over at Velvet as he turned the ignition and put the truck in reverse.

"Camping?"

"Yeah. How about it?"

"Now?"

He nodded. "I'll stop by the farm and grab a tent and sleeping bags. We'll be away from everything and everyone for the night."

That sounded wonderful to her. She needed that more than he could possibly know. It would just be one night, and she could deal with Vano, his scary cohorts, and the FBI tomorrow. She did want to get away, and right now letting Liam take care of everything sounded so tempting. Maybe they could work everything out, maybe she could relax and give her frayed nerves a rest, maybe she could even get some sleep. If there was one person on this earth right now that could make her feel safe, it was this man. "All right, yes. Let's do it."

He brushed his thumb over her lips. Then he jerked his chin. "Buckle up, baby."

CHAPTER TWENTY-EIGHT

Velvet sat on a blanket on the ground, looking out over the lights of Grand Junction shimmering in the distance. The early evening sky was a hazy purple and a big yellow moon hung low across the valley. The view was amazing with the entire valley spread out before them.

"It's stunning. How did you find this place?"

Liam had put up the small tent and built a fire. He sat next to her, unscrewed the cap on a pint of Fireball, and passed it over. "My brothers and I grew up around here. We've been coming up here camping and hiking for years. I know all the best spots."

She took the bottle eagerly and tipped it up. The flavor of Red Hots filled her mouth. It went down smooth and warmed her belly. She took a deep breath of the fresh mountain air and tried to relax. A couple more sips, and she felt her tight muscles loosen up. She rolled her head in an attempt to relieve the tension in her shoulders.

Liam cupped her shoulders and began kneading and massaging. She dropped her head, letting him work his magic. "God, that feels so good." He continued for a long while, until finally she felt the need to remind him why they'd come up here. "You wanted to talk?"

"Yeah, I did." His hands paused for a moment, and then resumed their ministrations. "Velvet, that night at the photo shoot… I overreacted. I should have listened to you; I should have given you the benefit of the doubt. I'm sorry I didn't."

She put her hand over his, stilling his movements. "I understand why you did what you did. I should have told you right from the beginning. It's all my fault."

He pulled her around to face him. "That's not true. We should have talked it out. I just flew off the handle. I regretted it almost immediately, but at the same time I wasn't sure if you were playing me for some reason."

"I wasn't, I swear to you."

He nodded. "None of it made sense. I'd come on to you, not the other way around, so how would you be setting me up for another con? Then when I read that article I felt like a complete jerk. I'd been so cruel to you. I'm sorry."

"It's all right. I understand."

"You forgive me?"

"Of course, if you can forgive me."

"Can we start over?"

She flew into his arms, hugging him tight. "Yes. Oh, God, yes. I've missed you so much."

"Me, too, baby." He buried his face in her neck and held her for a long time before finally pulling her arms from around his neck. He looked down at her, his hand coming up to cup her face. "I don't want you to be afraid to talk to me. I want you to feel like you can tell me anything."

"I want that, too."

"If we're in this, we're in this together, okay?"

Her eyes filled with happy tears, and she smiled up at him. "Okay."

He brushed the wetness from her cheeks. "So tell me about the trouble you're in."

Shame flooded through her. "I hate that I'm dragging you into this."

"Hey."

She lifted her head to look into his warm brown eyes.

"I want to be the one you tell your problems to,

the one you run to, the one you trust emphatically. I want to be *it* for you, Velvet, your everything."

"What are you saying?"

He took a breath and his brows rose. "I want to be your husband, the father of your children, and the only man you'll ever need for the rest of your life, if you'll have me. Does that spell it out enough, baby?"

"Oh, Liam."

"I love you, Velvet. I have since the moment you knocked on my door."

"I love you, too, Liam. I think I fell in love with you when I was fifteen. You were so sweet to me that day, like no one had ever been to me before."

He smiled. "Okay, then. We're going to figure this shit out, and then we're going to move on with our lives, and I promise you, baby, I'm going to give you the life you always wanted and make sure all those dreams you have come true."

She searched his eyes. "I know you will, because that's the kind of man you are. My instincts were right about you from that first day I walked into Brothers Ink. I believe in you, Liam. I always have."

"I'm going to make sure you don't ever regret it." He dipped his head and kissed her long and deep. It was a kiss full of love and emotion. When he pulled back he pressed his forehead to hers. "Now tell me everything and we'll figure it out together."

She gazed off at the city lights. "My brother was sent to prison a few years ago. He got out sometime last year."

Liam nodded. "Yeah, that's about when House of Crap popped up in town."

She shrugged. "I don't know why he picked Grand Junction to set up shop, especially with you guys as competition. It never made sense to me, but maybe there's another connection that brought him here, maybe one of those other guys—"

"Guys? What other guys?"

"He's got two men hanging around the shop. They're both ex-cons he met while he was in prison. I don't know much about them except they scare the hell out of me."

Liam's brows shot up. "Why didn't you tell me?" He surged to his feet. "Shit, Velvet, that settles it; there's no way in hell you're going back there."

She touched his jean-clad calf. "Liam, I've got to, the FBI—"

"Babe—"

"Please, sit down. Let me finish."

He complied and raked his hand through his hair impatiently. "Yeah, okay. Finish."

"Vano's been running cons since he was a teenager, but they were always small time." She shook her head, looking at the horizon, hating to admit this part but knowing she had to. She was determined never to hide anything from Liam again. She blew out a deep breath and met his eyes. "I overheard something at the shop and discovered he's been running a phone scam on senior citizens, conning them out of money. They've been sending it to him through the mail. A couple of days ago I went to the post office to get it from the box he keeps there. The FBI took me into custody on mail fraud charges."

"What? Are you serious?"

She nodded. "The penalty is up to twenty years in prison. The agent in charge presented me with a deal: total immunity if I cooperated and helped them get evidence against my brother and the others."

"Jesus Christ."

"There's more. When I bumped into you today, I'd just met the FBI agent at the diner around the corner."

Liam's eyes were intently focused on her. "And?"

"He told me Vano has multiple bank accounts for House of Ink and way more money is going through them than even what Vano's con is pulling in through the mail. A couple of days ago, they had me plant some bugs around the place and—"

"What?"

"It was part of the deal. He told me today they overheard some kind of shipment was coming in tomorrow, but they couldn't hear what it was. He wants me to try to find out."

"*You?* Are you kidding me?"

"They suspect drugs, possibly cocaine or heroin."

"Let me get this straight. The FBI thinks your brother is laundering drug money through his tattoo shop?"

"That's what Agent Sanders said."

"This just keeps getting better."

"I know my brother's done some bad shit, but he's never been involved with dealing drugs. Liam, no one knows my brother like I do, and maybe Vano's been a scammer all his life, but he's never been involved with drugs. He's always been a small time con man." She shook her head. "It just doesn't make sense."

Liam frowned. "Maybe he's gotten in over his head with these guys and can't see a way out."

She nodded. "Yes, maybe."

"Velvet if you go sticking your nose in these guys' business, who knows what they'll do if they catch you snooping around. You have to see the danger that puts you in."

"I know. I don't want to do it; I don't want to be involved with any of this, but what choice do I have?"

"Babe, there is no way in hell I'm letting you do this."

"I have to. If I don't, the immunity deal goes away. They caught me red handed, Liam. I opened the PO Box with the key and took the mail out. The payments Vano had scammed those people out of were in those envelopes. I'm looking at twenty years."

"Oh my God." Liam surged to his feet and began pacing. He dragged his palms down his face. "I'm gonna kill that son-of-a-bitch, Velvet. I mean it. I lay eyes on him again, he's dead."

"Liam—"

He whirled on her. "You better pray the FBI get him first."

She went to him, putting her hands on his chest. "Please, Liam, I don't want you to get involved. I couldn't bear it if something happened to you or if you did something that got you arrested, too."

"Baby, if you think I'm going to stand by and do nothing, you don't know me at all. They want to mess with the O'Rourke's, they're going to find out we don't play by the rules. Not when it comes to people we love."

She turned away and buried her face in her hands. "I'm so sorry I dragged you into all this. It was the last thing I wanted to do, but I feel like I'm trapped and there's no way out."

Liam stepped before her and pulled her hands away. When she wouldn't look at him, he tipped her face up with a finger under her chin. "We're in this together now, Velvet. Understand?"

She nodded. "Okay."

He searched her eyes a long time. "I think I've got a plan."

"You do? What?"

"We sneak in the shop after closing, and we tear the place apart. If that doesn't work I'll follow those guys and see where they go."

"We."

"Baby, I don't want you anywhere near them."

"You just said we were in this together."

"I don't want you hurt. I don't want you within a hundred miles of dangerous men like these.

That's final."

She saw the hard determination in his face. He meant every word. She loved that about him. She'd never in her life had a man that wanted to protect her and keep her safe like he did. The love she felt for him bubbled up and overwhelmed her. She cupped his face with her hands. "Liam?"

"I'm serious, Velvet."

"I know. But, Liam?"

He visibly relaxed at her acceptance of his declaration. "Yeah, baby?"

"Can we talk about it in the morning?" She dragged her thumb slowly across his bottom lip, hoping he'd take the hint. His eyes dropped to her mouth, and something shifted in his demeanor. His big hands closed over her hips, bringing her flush against him.

"Absolutely," he murmured as his mouth came down on hers.

***

Liam took her hand and led her into the tent. There wasn't a lot of room, so they both stripped, and he lay on the sleeping bags, grabbing her and pulling her on top.

He played with her clit until she was wet, then he

grasped her waist and lifted her, lowering her pussy onto his erection, slowly penetrating her silky softness. She moved on him, taking him farther inside, inch by inch, and the feeling was incredible.

His hands tightened, holding her in place as he watched her pussy stretch around him. "Christ, I love watching you take me."

She rocked up and down, undulating against him.

He lay back, content to watch this sexy-as-hell show she didn't even realize she was putting on for him. Fuck, it was sheer torture watching her work her body against his, seeking out her orgasm.

"Oh, God, Liam," she breathed and began moving faster and faster. "I can't..."

"Keep going, baby." He thrust his hips up and grabbed both her bouncing breasts in his hands, squeezing them and pinching her nipples.

She looked down at him with half-lidded eyes, her mouth open and panting.

"Jesus, sweetness, you are so gorgeous."

He dipped a hand, his thumb moving circles over her clit, and she clenched down on his cock, driving him fucking crazy. He couldn't last much longer. Her pussy was squeezing him so tight, and the sight of her bouncing on his dick sent him over the edge. He gripped her hips tight and pounded into her.

Velvet arched her back and tensed her body as she came on him.

It was a beautiful thing to watch. The vulnerability written on her face called out to him, and he came hard, his hips lifting off the ground.

She collapsed on top of him, and his arms went around her, catching her to his chest and letting her know he'd always be there.

"Liam." She sank down over him like a deflated soufflé.

There was so much in that one word and in the way she melted against him. She was giving in to the safety of his arms; she was giving everything over to him, all the problems, all the worries, and she was trusting in him. He knew in that moment everything would be fine.

For the longest time, she didn't move. He'd lie there and hold her as long as she wanted.

Finally, when her body stopped pulsing around his dick, he rolled her to her back and leaned over her, giving little licks to her nipples until he'd drawn every last shudder from her.

Liam tenderly brushed her hair from her face and traced his fingertip over her temple, cheek, and down her delicate jaw. "I didn't know it was possible, but you look even more beautiful."

She turned sleepy eyes to him, but even then, he could see the worry descending over her.

He searched her eyes and ran his thumb over the furrows in her forehead. "I don't want you to worry about anything, baby. Okay?"

She stroked his bearded face. "I'm starting to believe that maybe there is a way out of all of this, Liam."

"There is, Velvet, and we're going to find it. I promise." He kissed her forehead. "You're safe, baby. Get some sleep."

Her eyes slid closed, and she slept for the first time in week.

***

Skin's head snapped around to Weasel. "Where is she?"

"I'm pulling up the app; give me a second, will ya?"

The tattoo shop was closed and the shades drawn. Cooter and Finn had gone home ten minutes ago. Skin's gaze swiveled back to where

Vano stood by the register. "I told you to keep a close eye on her, goddamn it."

"She left this afternoon to run to the store. Said she was on the rag and had to get some tampons. What was I supposed to do, tell her no? Go fuckin' get 'em myself, for Christ's sake?"

"And now your fucking key's missing; you think that's a coincidence? You're such a fucking moron." He paced, lighting a cigarette.

"Maybe she's home now," Vano suggested.

Skin jabbed the index finger of the hand that held the burning cigarette in Vano's direction. "You think I didn't just come from there? You think I'm stupid. Ain't nobody there. Ain't nobody been there either."

Vano ran his hand through his hair. "She's around somewhere. She'll turn up. She's got no car."

Skin turned back to Weasel. "You find her yet?"

"Bingo."

"Where is she?"

"Not in town, that's for sure."

"What do you mean?"

"Give me a second, this map's hard to see." He put his thumb and forefinger on the screen and enlarged the area, zooming in on the flashing red dot. He snickered. "This app for finding your cell phone" —he paused to look at Vano—"or in this case your sister's cell phone, is cool as hell. Good thing Skin made you download it to her phone when she wasn't looking."

"Just tell me where the hell she is!"

"I'm trying to read it. The type's pretty damn small. She's in this green area outside of town. National Monument Park, near one of the campgrounds. Hey, this thing's pretty damn accurate. How 'bout that?"

"That remains to be seen. We gotta find her first." Skin grabbed Vano by the shirt and shook him. "You better pray we find her!"

"What would she be doing up there?" Weasel asked Vano.

"Hell, I don't know. Maybe she's out there with that guy from Brothers Ink. She'll come back. What are you so upset about?"

"Because we got product coming in tomorrow, and I don't want any surprises. I don't trust her. I like to keep tabs on people I don't trust. I like to know where all the players in the game are, and if she goes to the cops, we could be walking into a trap tomorrow, and I ain't going back to prison."

CHAPTER TWENTY-NINE

Skin and Weasel drove slowly up into the east entrance of the park, climbing higher and higher. The two-lane road wound precariously with sheer drops on the right and views that went on for miles.

Skin parked the van, sat behind the wheel, and stared out at the trail, barely visible in the darkness. The cockeyed sign that read *campsites* pointed to the right. Dawn was starting to lighten the horizon. He glanced over at Weasel. "This it?"

Weasel pulled up the tracker on the screen of his phone. They both watched the pinging of the signal that proved she was close.

Skin shut the engine off. "Let's go."

"Shit, I told you I ain't goin' out there in the dark. There are mountain lions up here. Fuck that."

Skin leaned forward and opened the glove box, pulling out a handgun. He drew the slide back, chambered a round, and then shouldered his door open. "Come on you fucking pussy."

Weasel cursed, shoved his door open, and climbed out. He followed Skin down the trail.

***

Liam felt the warm lush skin of Velvet's naked body snuggle up against him, and he smiled even before he cracked his eyes open. His hand stroked up her back, then down to squeeze her amazing ass. She rubbed against him, and his dick hardened. Seems anytime she was near, it came to life; having her naked against him was really getting its attention. The warmth of the sleeping bag and tent was like a wonderful cocoon against the chill of the morning.

"I have to pee," Velvet whispered.

Liam chuckled, his chest bouncing her head. "Now? I was just about to roll you over and do all sorts off sinfully decadent things to you."

"You'll have to wait a few minutes." She wiggled out of the bag, put his flannel shirt on over her bare breasts, and slid into her jeans and boots.

Liam rose up on an elbow, grabbed the back of her neck, and hauled her down for a quick kiss before releasing her. "Hurry back, babe."

She crawled to the exit, and Liam lay down; his eyes drifting shut, only to pop open again when she stuck her head back through the opening in the tent. "You know, some coffee would be amazing."

"Damn, you're a demanding wench first thing in the morning," he grumbled.

"Pleaseeee." She gave him an entreating smile, and with her tousled hair, she'd never looked more appealing.

"I'll see what I can do, beautiful."

She blew him a kiss and left.

Liam stretched, then pulled his jeans on and slipped his thermal shirt over his head. He yanked on his boots and emerged from the tent. The edge of the horizon was a light purple with just a tinge of pink. It reflected across the cloudy sky like a watercolor painting. He never got tired of the beauty of the Grand Valley.

Moving to the remains of the fire, he squatted down to poke at the smoldering embers with a stick and then tossed some kindling on top. With a squirt from the small can of lighter fluid he'd brought, it flared to life. He piled on some medium size branches and soon the fire was crackling and licking the wood with flames of orange.

He dug in the pack he'd brought for the small fry pan and a blue enamel coffee mug. He uncapped a water bottle and poured some in the pan, then set it on top of the logs to boil. Then he dug out a piece of cotton cheesecloth and put it over the cup, making a well and securing it to the rim with a rubber band. He dug out a baggie of coffee grounds, inhaling the rich aroma, and shook a portion into the well of the cloth.

The water in the shallow pan was soon boiling. He grabbed a glove from inside the pack and used it as an oven mitt to pull the pan from the fire. After letting it cool for a minute, he poured it carefully over the grounds until the cup was almost full. Setting the pan back in the fire with some more water, he took the cloth off the cup and brought it to his lips. Grinning, he murmured, "McGyver, you got nothin' on me."

***

Velvet squatted down to pee. It was quiet with not even the call of a bird, nothing but the sound of the wind howling up the mountain. She felt a prickle on the back of her neck and the feeling that someone was watching her snaked up her spine like cold fingers.

She'd trudged a good ways from the tent, and now she was regretting going that distance. Quickly tugging her pants back up, she searched through the pines for the orange of the tent. Craning her neck, a small bit of the bright colored nylon fabric became visible in the distance.

She took a few steps and was grabbed from behind. As she sucked in a breath, a hand clamped over her mouth and the cold steel of a gun barrel pressed to her temple.

"Stay quiet or I'll blow your fucking brains out, Velvet," a familiar voice whispered in her ear.

Skin! What the hell was he doing up here?

She heard a quiet snicker from behind her off to her left. Skin wasn't alone. That had to be his partner in crime, Weasel. The two were joined at the hip.

"Not a sound. You understand me?" Skin growled.

She nodded her head, her mouth still clamped tight in his hold.

"You come up here with your new boyfriend, huh? Did you give that pussy of yours to him?"

She was afraid to answer, so she didn't move.

"From now on, ain't nobody gonna be touching that pussy but me. And I'm gonna kill that motherfucker for touching what's mine."

Velvet's stomach dropped at the thought of Liam. She didn't want him hurt. She'd do anything to prevent it. She whimpered behind his hand.

"Told you, not a fucking sound!" he hissed, shaking her.

She nodded, frantic to appease him.

"Maybe I'll fuck you right here, right now," Skin whispered, grinding his pelvis into her ass.

He was getting off on tormenting her with his threats. She could feel his erection and it sickened her.

"That dude's gonna come," Weasel whined softly. "Let's get out of here."

"Shut up," Skin snapped in a low growl. His attention returned to Velvet and his mouth pressed against the shell of her ear. "Did you tell him? Did you tell your fucking boyfriend what you know?"

She shook her head.

"I'm not stupid. I know you've been snooping around. You think I don't know?" Then he pushed her forward toward the campsite.

***

Liam eyed the horizon again and wondered what was taking Velvet so long. He stood as the cracking of a twig sounded behind him. "I was just gonna come look—"

He broke off as he turned and found himself staring at a shaking, terrified Velvet, her neck in the headlock of a scary, tattooed skinhead who was holding a gun to her head.

"I saved you the trouble. Here she is," he said with a sneer.

A chuckle brought Liam's eyes to the weasely dude standing to the guy's left. He had 'side-kick' written all over him, from the way he stood a step back, to his weaponless hands, to the way his nervous gaze kept shifting to the man with the gun.

Liam dismissed him as not being much of a threat and returned his attention to the man holding Velvet.

"What do you want, Skin?" Velvet whispered.

Liam's eyes narrowed. She knew him. These two had to be the ex-cons working for Vano. She'd been right to be afraid of them.

Liam immediately began to assess the list of weapons he had within reach: the knife in his pack, the pan of boiling water on the fire, the stack of wood, and maybe even the can of lighter fluid.

"You shouldn't have taken off, my little honey-pot."

"I'm not your honey-pot. I'm not your anything," Velvet insisted in a hiss.

"Oh, just you wait." He stroked the muzzle of

the gun along her cheek. "You and me are going to be spending a lot of time together."

Hot rage ran through Liam's veins. He wanted to tear this guy limb from limb.

Velvet took that moment to fling her head back, smashing it into Skin's nose. He staggered, releasing her to grab his face. Weasel stood stock still, staring at the blood pouring from Skin's nose and mouth as Velvet darted toward Liam.

Liam grabbed the hot pan and flung it. The scalding water splattered over Skin's face, and the red-hot pan hit the side of Weasel's. Both howled in pain.

Liam didn't waste a second. He slung his pack over his shoulder and grabbed Velvet by the hand. They ran from the campsite, down the slope toward the ridge. It was rocky-going in the dim light. They headed toward the rim that overlooked the valley.

The branches of Juniper trees tore at their arms. Velvet slid on the loose rock, but Liam tightened his grip on her hand, keeping her on her feet. They hurried on. Liam frantically studied the landscape. He and his brothers had been up here many times; he knew there was a way down to his right, if he could just find it. There were many dangers in the park—snakes, big cats, scorpions even, but right now the biggest threat to their lives were the men he could hear pursuing them. Weasel was cursing and both were making a lot of noise.

Liam found the rock outcropping he'd been searching for, the one he remembered finding as a boy. It had an overhanging formation and a hidden recessed area beneath it. It was steep and dangerous to get down to, but if they could get under it, perhaps they could evade the men. Liam was resourceful and determined to protect Velvet at all costs, but they were out gunned, and he knew their best bet was to hide, not to run.

He turned to Velvet as the sound of the men pursuing them got closer. "This is steep. Hold on tight to me."

She nodded and clung to his arm. He slid a few feet down on the loose rock and climbed into the small cave, Velvet right behind him. Below them was a steep slope. Off to the left was sheer rock. The only way in and out was to the right.

Liam put his finger to his mouth, and Velvet nodded, going completely silent. He slipped the pack quietly from his shoulder and dug his hunting knife out. It wasn't the wisest thing to bring a knife to a gunfight, but it was all he had. He only hoped the men would either become completely disoriented and get lost or lose their trail. They waited quietly, barely breathing. Liam swore silently when he heard voices approaching.

"Which way did they go?"

"I don't know, dipshit. Look for 'em. They're here somewhere."

"Fuck, that's a long way down."

Liam glanced at Velvet who was looking up and then at him with wide eyes. The men were right above them on the rocky outcropping. He pointed up, and she nodded.

"My face is blistering. Fuck it hurts," Weasel whined. "Let's go back."

"We're not fucking going back. I'm gonna kill that motherfucker, and then I'm gonna fuck that bitch right here on the ground." Skin's voice sounded strange with his broken nose.

"You're bleedin' bad, Skin. Let's just go back. We can get them when they get to their truck."

"I said no."

They heard the sound of loose rock scratching across the ground. A couple of stones dropped over the edge and sailed past the cave opening toward the bottom of the canyon.

"Fuck, I almost fucking fell! They ain't here, Skin. Let's go back. It's steep as hell. I don't want to fall off this fucking rim."

"I thought you had guts."

"Yeah, and I'd like to keep them in my body, not splattered all over the canyon floor."

"Shut up, dickhead. I think they're down there."

"Where?"

Liam felt a tug on his sleeve and looked at Velvet. She was bug-eyed and pointing. It was still dim light, but he could see the outline of the big cat, off to the right of them about twenty yards. The mountain lion stared right at him, and Liam could only imagine it believed it had its breakfast cornered in the small cave, but Liam knew there wasn't much room on this ledge, and as the cat eyed the ground below, he hoped it was realizing it would be a dangerous jump if it lost its footing.

There was a sound above them, and the cat's gaze shifted to the men up on the rocky outcropping. It sniffed the air. Liam supposed it smelled all that blood that was probably pouring from Skin's busted nose. He watched the cat closely and said a silent prayer, tightening his grip on the knife. Apparently the animal decided the men above would be a much easier catch, and it bound toward them, leaping with ease. It went out of sight, sailing above them with a growl he knew he'd never forget.

Blood-curdling screams and the shuffling of feet filled the air. A clattering sound hit the rocks and they watched the handgun fly over the edge of the cliff.

The screaming continued, and the sounds of struggle carried through the morning air. There was a thud, and Weasel tumble over the edge, falling past them to certain death. His terrified scream ended with a distant thump.

Liam peered over the edge to see the broken body lying on the canyon floor.

The screams above them cut off with a gurgling sound and then the sound of a thick body against dirt and rocks grew softer in the distance. The cat must've been dragging his prey into the trees.

Liam was armed with nothing but that knife, but he couldn't let that man, no matter how much he deserved it, be eaten alive by that cat. He moved to the sloping rock and took a few steps out of the cave, peering over the outcropping. He was in time to see the cat dragging Skin's lifeless body backward, the man's jugular torn open. As he watched the man's legs disappear into the vegetation, he knew there was no hope of saving him.

Liam moved back into the cave. He had to get Velvet to safety in case the cat came back.

She stood with her hand over her mouth, tears in her eyes. He pulled her into his arms and hugged her tight, stroking her head. "It's over. You're okay." He held her for what seemed like a long time, but was probably in reality only a few moments. When he relaxed his hold, she looked up at him.

"Are they dead?"

He cupped her face and nodded. "We have to save ourselves, babe. There's nothing we can do for them. We need to get out of here. Are you going to be okay?"

She shook her head. She was panicking, he realized; the men, the sheer drop, the terrifying cat, it was all too much. He understood why this strong, tough girl of his was having a hard time holding it together; anyone would.

"We'll find a route up," he assured her. He dug in his pack and pulled out a length of rope. "I'm gonna tie the rope to you and then secure it to me. The terrain is steep, and if you look down it can be scary, so don't."

"You're freaking me out."

He quickly tied the rope around his waist and then hers, yanking the knot tight with a jerk. "Babe, I don't want you to start worrying too much; I want you to concentrate on what you're doing. Watch your footing and hang onto me."

"Liam—"

"Velvet, you have to trust me. You have no choice."

"I trust you."

"Ok, sweetheart, let's do this. Follow my exact steps, and you'll be good. Stay on the mossy parts, that way you won't slip on loose rock."

She did as he told her, and he'd never been prouder of her. They made it back up the slope to more level ground. Moving to the right, giving that cat a wide berth, wherever it was, he led her toward the campground.

They jogged the whole way, making it to where the truck and tent were.

When Velvet made a beeline for the truck, Liam brought her up short and grabbed her face. "Baby, I know you want to get out of here, but we've got to take everything with us—every trace of evidence we've been here. I don't want anything tying us to those two men's deaths.

She nodded. "Okay. You're right."

He jerked the rope off them. "Come on, we need to move quickly."

They gathered everything and loaded it all.

"Get in the truck, Velvet."

She did as he ordered while he grabbed a small shovel out of the truck bed and buried the fire over with dirt. He tossed the shovel into the back and jumped behind the wheel to turn the truck out onto the road. Once on the pavement, he returned, grabbed up a branch and rubbed out the tire tracks and any footprints as he backed his way to the pavement. Tossing the branch aside, he stared at the site. All that went through his head was that there are a dozen mistakes made at any crime scene. He knew he and Velvet had committed no crime, but he didn't want them to be connected to this shit in any way. He jumped behind the wheel and high-tailed it out of there.

The cab of the truck was filled with tense silence as they descended down Rim Rock Road. He studied Velvet. She seemed about as shell-shocked as he was, and he knew he had to take charge of this. "Here's what we have to do…"

At his words, she looked over at him.

"We weren't here. We didn't see anything. We don't know anything about what happened to those men. Got it?"

She nodded.

"They got what they deserved."

She nodded again.

"Babe, talk to me. You okay?" He squeezed her hand. When she continued to just stare out the window at the scenery passing by, he tugged her over. "Come here."

She scooted across the seat and under his waiting arm, which closed tight around her. He rubbed up and down her upper arm. "Everything's gonna be okay. I'm not gonna let anyone hurt you. Understand?"

She nodded and tucked in against him.

He drove the rest of the way down the twisting, turning road one-handed. It was challenging, but there was no way he was taking his arm from around her.

CHAPTER THIRTY

Liam didn't pull his arm from around Velvet until he spun the wheel up the driveway to the farmhouse.

She straightened. "What are we doing?"

He parked the truck. "We're going inside. We're going to take a shower and clean up. We're going to wash our clothes and get rid of any evidence we've been up there. I'm putting the camping gear back where it was." He glanced at the clock. It was ten minutes past seven. "What time does the shop open up?"

"Not 'till eleven."

"When does Vano go in?"

"Usually not until ten, but nothing's usual anymore."

"We could wait until tonight, but we may be too late by then. I say we hit the place now and tear it apart, see what we can find."

"I don't know."

"We'll do a drive by and make sure he's not

there."

"Okay."

Liam reached for the door handle. "Come on, angel."

They climbed from the truck, and Liam put his arm around her and led her inside.

Mrs. Larsen was up taking a pan of cinnamon rolls out of the oven. She turned when they entered. "Well, Liam. I wasn't expecting you this morning. What a nice surprise."

"Mrs. Larsen, this is my fiancée, Velvet." He smiled down at her, and she looked back at him with the first smile she'd given him since she crawled out of the tent this morning.

"Your fiancée? Why I had no idea you'd gotten engaged! Congratulations!"

"Well, I haven't put a ring on her finger yet, but I asked her last night."

"While you were up camping? Why, isn't that romantic?"

Liam exchanged a look with Velvet, and they both realized there were people who knew they'd gone camping. He glanced back at Mrs. Larsen. "We're going to go upstairs and get cleaned up, then some of those rolls would sure taste good."

"Well, all righty. You two do that, and I'll have breakfast ready in a jiffy."

Liam led Velvet upstairs to the bathroom. He turned on the shower. "It'll take a minute to heat up. It's an old house. Get undressed, and I'll be right back."

She nodded and he moved down the hall. He grabbed clean clothes from those he kept in his old room. Then he tapped on Maxwell and Malee's door. "Max, you in there?"

Maxwell opened the door and stuck his head out. "Liam? What are you doing here?"

"Took Velvet up camping last night. We're gonna take a shower. Any chance Malee's got something Velvet can wear? I mean I know they aren't the same height, but maybe a sundress or something might fit her."

"Yeah, give me a minute."

"You come up with anything, just leave it outside the bathroom door, and I'll get it."

"Sure, man. So, how'd it go?"

"Get dressed, and I'll tell you over breakfast."

"Deal."

Liam walked back to the bathroom, closing the door quietly. Velvet was already behind the shower curtain and steam was beginning to fill the room. He set his change of clothes down on the lid of the toilet, then reached between his shoulder blades and pulled his thermal shirt over his head. He tossed it to the floor and shucked his boots and jeans. "How's the water?"

"Heavenly," she replied as he drew the curtain aside and stepped in. She was facing the water spray. His eyes swept over her back and ass. She was slender and yet had all the right curves. He moved in close, putting his hands on her tiny waist and moving over her hips. She leaned into him, her skin hot from the steamy water. His arms slid around her, and his mouth dropped to the wet skin where her neck met the curve of her shoulder. He pressed soft open-mouthed kisses along it.

Her head dropped back, and his mouth moved up to her ear. "This is the first shower we've taken together."

"I think you're right," she murmured.

"Give me the soap." His hands closed over hers, taking the bar from her. When his palms were lathered, he set the bar on the shower caddy hanging from the showerhead. Moving with care, he soaped her wet glistening skin from her throat to her waist, at first avoiding her breasts and making her squirm in anticipation, and then closing over them and giving her what she wanted. He gave them all his attention until the tension in her muscles melted off her. He knew her brain was buzzing with all that had happened, and he wanted to give her a few minutes relief.

He dropped one hand, trailing down her stomach and delving between her legs. He swirled the soapy slickness all over her and stroked and moved his fingers in tight circles around her clit. He kept at it until she writhed against him. When she was close to coming, he pinched her nipple, and she groaned out a shout as she trembled with orgasm.

His mouth hovered over the shell of her ear. "I love you, Velvet."

"Oh…Liam," she whispered, biting her lip and trying to hold back the moan that vibrated in her throat. When her shudders finally ceased, her forehead fell against the side of his neck, and she gasped out a breathy, "I love you, too, Liam. So much."

He gathered her in his arms and moved her against the wall. "Brace your hands."

She did as he told her, placing her palms on the

tile as he positioned himself and speared into her slick wetness.

Her head fell forward, and she went up on her toes. He couldn't tear his eyes from her gorgeous, firm, perfect ass that jutted out toward him. Only thing better was the way her slick pussy took his dick as he pumped in and out of her. Fucking beautiful. He moved one palm up her back from the two dimples at the base, up over the tattoo he'd put between her shoulder blades—the stallion they'd seen that day they'd gone for a hike. *Wild and Free,* were the words tattooed in a banner underneath the design. That's what she'd always be to him, and he intended to make sure she stayed that way. He'd die before he let anything happen to her, and he sure as hell wasn't letting any FBI agent send her to prison.

The resolve strengthened within him, and his thrusts accelerated along with it. He moved in close against her, his left palm landing on the tile next to hers while his right arm locked tight around her waist. He dipped his head alongside hers and pumped hard. He knew he was getting close, but he wanted her right there with him. His mouth hovered over her ear, and he whispered, "Touch yourself."

She did, automatically following his command, as

if she were powerless to do anything but as he wished.

He dropped his mouth to her shoulder and nipped, growling softly, "I'm close, baby, so close. Get yourself there."

She moaned, her fingers working her clit.

He dropped his hand from the tile and pinched her nipple as he sucked hard on her neck. She moaned again, her body shuddering in orgasm, and his arm tightened. He thrust into her and exploded in release.

He slid slowly in and out of her slick pussy a couple more times and then wrapped his arms around her, holding her close.

Her hand came up to cup his cheek, and she turned her face against his neck and kissed him. "I love you, Liam."

Euphoria expanded through his body. After a moment, he pulled out, and she turned in his arms. "I think we need to soap up again."

He grinned down at her. "Yeah, and in this old house, we better be quick before we run out of hot water."

"Thank you." She stared up at him, her expression turning serious.

He frowned, and kissed the tip of her nose. "For what?"

"For believing in me, for coming for me yesterday, for loving me, for saving my life today. For all of it."

"I told you, you're it for me." He stroked the side of her face with his thumb. "Today, tomorrow, forever. Understand?"

She smiled, and nodded.

"You and me, together against the world."

She chuckled. "The world doesn't stand a chance."

He returned her laughter, glad to see happiness back on her face, if even for a moment. "No, it doesn't."

***

Once they dried off, Liam opened the bathroom door and found a small stack of folded clothes. He grabbed them and stepped into the steamy room, holding them out to Velvet.

She frowned. "What's that?"

"I asked if you could borrow some fresh clothes from Max's wife, Malee."

"Is she the one in the picture I saw framed on the wall?"

He nodded.

"Liam, she's lovely, but she's about four inches shorter than me."

"Well, at least take a look."

Velvet picked up the folded item on top and held it up. It was a long pretty floral sundress. It probably was to Malee's ankles, but it only came to just below Velvet's knees. She slipped it over her head. It fit her chest and waist and hips and hung in a loose flowing style. "How does it look?"

"Beautiful," Liam said, his eyes moving over her and stopping on her chest. "You look good braless."

"I have a bra. It got shoved in with the sleeping bag when we were in such a hurry to leave."

"Yeah, I may have to hide all your bras."

"Liam!"

"I liked seeing you wearing my flannel shirt this morning, too."

"I liked wearing it." She picked it up off the bathroom floor. "After we wash it, I might just steal it from you."

"What's mine is yours, sweetheart."

A few minutes later they gathered around the big round oak table in the kitchen. Mrs. Larsen had a plate of bacon set in the middle next to the cinnamon rolls, and she was making her way around, spooning up helpings of scrambled eggs on each plate.

Liam sat next to Velvet. He reached over and squeezed her hand.

Max and Malee sat across from them, Malee with her obvious baby bump.

"Where's my little nephew?" Liam asked.

"The school bus picked him up while you were in the shower," Max said.

Liam made the introductions. "Velvet, this is my brother's wife, Malee."

She extended her hand. "Pleased to meet you. I hope we're not inconveniencing you by dropping by like this so early."

Malee smiled. "Not at all. You are most welcome."

"When is your baby due?"

"In eight weeks." Malee dropped a hand to her belly.

"You must be so excited."

"Yes. And ready for her to be here."

"It's a girl?"

She nodded.

"Do you have a name picked out?"

Malee looked up at her husband. Max answered for her. "We haven't decided yet."

"Yes, we have," she insisted.

"We're down to two options."

Malee rolled her eyes. "We've decided."

"We've decided not to share it until the big day."

"Well, I'm sure she'll be beautiful."

"Thank you."

"So, you two seem to be getting along great from the sounds of it," Max commented.

"From the sounds of it?" Liam asked, biting into a gooey roll.

"Thin walls, bro."

Velvet covered her mouth with her hand. "Oh, my God."

"Don't be an ass, Max." Liam gave him a look as he licked the icing from his thumb.

"She's gonna be a part of this family, she's gonna have to get used to the teasing. Besides, I get the feeling she's a tough one."

"I can handle it." Velvet lifted her chin.

Max grabbed the plate of bacon and dropped a couple pieces on Velvet's plate. "By the way, I'm sorry for the way I acted that day you came to the shop."

"I understand."

Liam frowned. "Wait, what? When was this?

How'd you act?"

"The day she came and gave Jameson that check. I was kind of a dick to her." He glared at Liam. "On your behalf, of course."

"What'd you do?"

"I just told her she had no business there, and she should go."

"Really?"

"Yeah. Then Ava told me to sit down and shut up."

Liam grinned, his coffee mug halfway to his mouth. "She's a wise woman."

Max winked at Velvet. "That she is. She was the only one of us who gave Velvet the benefit of the doubt straight off the bat."

They ate quickly and said their goodbyes, making excuses that Velvet had an appointment. Fifteen minutes later, Liam was cruising slowly past the front of House of Ink. He turned the corner, and they rolled down a side street. He peered down the alley that ran behind the businesses but saw no cars this early, just a garbage truck down on the end.

He looked over at Velvet craning her neck to see out the back window. "What do you think?"

"Let's try it."

Liam cut the wheel and made a U-turn. He pulled

to the curb on the side street and jammed the gearshift in park. He studied Velvet. "You ready?"

"Yes."

"You have a key?"

She nodded. "I swiped one off Vano's key chain the morning I met the FBI agent. By now he probably figures I have it."

"Then let's be quick."

They jogged to the back of the business, and Liam kept an eye out while Velvet unlocked the heavy metal door. They weren't two feet inside, the door shutting behind them, when a beeping sound went off. Liam's eyes hit a security panel on the wall. "Shit, babe. You know the code?"

"Fuck. No."

"What would be easy for him to remember?"

"His birthday, maybe."

"Try it, quick. We've only got about thirty seconds."

She punched it in, but the screen still flashed red. "Shit."

"Anything else you can try?"

She bit her lip. "Wait." She punched in another number and the screen turned green.

"Bingo."

"What'd you use?"

"My mother's birthday."

"He a momma's boy, huh?" Liam asked.

"Totally."

Liam pulled her to him and kissed her forehead. "Good thinking, babe. Let's get to work."

"His office is in here." She led him down the hall to the first door on the right and fumbled with the lock. It opened, and Liam flipped the light on. The desk was a mess with an overflowing ashtray, bottles of ink, rubbing alcohol, used cotton wipes, an ear piercing gun that looked like someone was in the process of cleaning, old tattoo magazines, manila files piled haphazardly, and papers scattered.

His eyes moved around the room, landing on the small safe on the floor behind the desk. "You know the combination?"

She shook her head. "I can't get in the safe."

"You sure? You did so well with the security system."

She smirked at him, and he grinned back.

"You check the desk, I'll go through this file cabinet," Velvet said.

"Doesn't look like he uses it much," Liam joked, eyeing the mess on the desk.

She rolled her eyes.

Liam pushed aside a stack and pulled out the new issue of Inked Up, the one with them on the cover. "Velvet."

She looked over. He held it up. Her mouth dropped open, and she took it, staring down at the cover. "Oh my God."

"Pretty awesome, right?"

She thumbed through it, taking in the photographs of the article. "They're good."

Liam took the magazine from her. "They're more than good. But wait, there's more." He flipped to the article on her and watched her reaction as she saw the black and white picture of herself and the article banner. Her eyes moved along the words.

"What does it say?"

He told her and watched her eyes fill. "It's a good story, baby. Don't cry."

She flipped it closed and nodded, then frowned. "How does Vano have this?"

"Good question."

"He must have taken it from my mail."

"He's probably been looking for you, and his key, I'm guessing. He's probably searched your room."

"How do you think those two goons found us?"

Liam shook his head. "No clue. You think they put a tracker on you? Because if they'd followed us, I don't think they would have waited until morning."

"A tracking device? That's creepy." She frowned. "Shit."

"What?"

"I wonder if the FBI has one on me."

Liam's jaw tightened at the thought. "Let's get to work. I don't want to be here long."

She nodded and moved to the file cabinet. Liam scanned the folders, finding the usual stuff, print outs of payroll, electric bills, phone bills. He found one buried at the bottom, labeled *Advertising*. He thought that was strange since he knew they did no advertising, at least he'd never seen any in the time the place had existed. He flipped it open. It was a single page with a list of acronyms in a column and a large number next to each. BOC, CBOC, CB&T. And then they all clicked into place. These were banks: Bank of Colorado, Community Bank of Colorado, Colorado Bank & Trust. He scanned the numbers next to each. They didn't look like account numbers, they looked like amounts with commas. "Jesus Christ."

"What?" Velvet glanced up.

He showed her the list. "I think those are the amounts he has in each bank."

She skimmed the page. "Shit, that's a lot of money. No way he got all that from a phone scam."

"You sure?"

"There's no way. Not unless he had a room full of people working for him full time." She closed the file drawer. "There's nothing in this cabinet."

"Keep looking."

Her eyes scanned the room. "Wait. What's that?"

Liam twisted to look. There was a small duffle bag on the floor behind the desk with a coat half thrown over it. She squatted down and unzipped it. They both stared down at three plastic wrapped bricks of what looked like brown sugar. Their eyes met and Liam said, "I'm guessing that's heroin. I think you'd better call your friend at the FBI."

Velvet's eyes widened and flashed over his shoulder. That was the last thing he saw as his head exploded in pain, and he crumpled to the floor.

CHAPTER THIRTY-ONE

Velvet screamed and clutched Liam to her as she stared up at Vano. He had a gun pointed right at her face. "What are you doing, Vano?!"

"I should be asking *you* that, Vee. I heard what he said. You were going to call your friend at the FBI. Since when do you have friends at the FBI, Vee? Huh? And where the hell have you been? Skin and Weasel went out looking for you. Did they find you?"

She stayed quiet, not wanting to answer any of those questions. She clutched Liam and ran her hand over his head. There was a lump forming on the back of his skull, but she didn't feel any blood. Still, he could have a serious concussion, and it worried her that he still hadn't come around. "Liam? Liam, please wake up."

"Liam, Liam wake up," Vano parodied her attempts. "You sound like a love-sick kid, like you did back in Indiana that summer."

"Shut up, Vano! I found the drugs! I know what you've been up to with Skin and Weasel! You're dealing aren't you?"

"What I do with Skin and Weasel ain't none of your business, and if you know what's good for you, you better keep your fucking mouth shut! And what's this shit about calling the FBI? I hope that was a joke, Vee. Because Skin will kill you, deader than a doornail if you even say that shit."

Velvet studied her brother. He looked disheveled and sweat was pouring down his face. His skin was sallow, and his hair was greasy. She'd never seen him like this before. Vano was always concerned about his appearance. He was always well dressed, and he took extra care with his hair, even using hairspray and products on it. He liked to consider himself a real ladies man, a player, but now he just looked like a two-bit tweeker. "Are you using, Vano?"

He jammed a cigarette in his mouth and flicked a lighter open, dipping to light up.

Her eyes dropped to the gun he still held in his right hand. Would he use that on her? Would he really shoot his own sister over drug money? She glanced down in the duffle. It was a lot of drugs, and there was a lot of money in those accounts. So, yeah, he probably would shoot her.

He took a deep drag. "It's none of your business what I do, just like it hasn't seemed to be your concern what happens with Ma. You've never loved her, have you?"

His sudden change in topic had her reeling. He had to be using. He was jittery, and his eyes darted around like he was paranoid.

He pointed the gun at her again. "Who were you gonna call, Vee, huh? Tell me!"

"I wasn't going to call anyone, I swear." Looking down the barrel of a gun was terrifying—just as scary as staring at that mountain lion about to pounce. "You have to believe me."

"I don't have to do shit." The barrel shifted aim to Liam's back. "And what's that motherfucker doing here? He's got no business in my shop, Vee! You fucking him now? Skin's not gonna be too happy about that. He wants you, you know that? He plans to have you, and I won't be able to stop him." He was rambling again, and he began pacing, sucking on that cigarette.

"Vano, please. Just let us leave."

He whirled on her. "I can't let you leave. Don't you see? Skin will be back soon."

Velvet swallowed, and her eyes shifted to the door. She wondered if she should tell him that Skin was dead. Would he believe her? Would he be angry? "Vano, please, put down the gun and let's talk."

"Talk? You want to talk? About what? About what a lousy sister you've been, about how I've had to take care of mom all these years, about how you abandoned us? What do you want to talk about, Vee?" he screamed.

"We can talk about all of that. I'm so sorry I wasn't here for you, Vano. Just…put the gun down. I'm your sister; you don't need the gun to make me do anything. Please, Vano."

"Yeah, I do, Vee. You think you're so smart. You think you got this all figured out." He made a swirling motion with the gun. "You've got nothin' figured out. You don't know shit about me and what I've had to deal with. You think prison was easy? I did what I did because that's the way I was raised. Pops raised me to be the man of the family. When he died, that's what I did." He slammed his palm on his chest. "You're the one who didn't do what she was supposed to!" There were tears in his eyes now.

"I'm sorry, Vano."

He whirled and pointed the gun at her. "No you're

not! You're not, Vee! You have never been sorry! But you're gonna be. Get up!"

"What?" Her arms tightened around Liam.

"Let go of him and get up!"

"What are you going to do?"

"What I should have done a long time ago." He grabbed her arm and hauled her across the linoleum, dragging her out of the office and into the tiny bathroom. He yanked her to the sink that jutted from the wall and pulled a pair of handcuffs from his pants pocket. Before she realized what he was going to do, he had her cuffed to the big curving pipe under the sink.

She tugged on her arm. "Goddamn it, Vano, let me go!"

He backed away. "Who's the smart one now, Vee?" He disappeared into his office where Liam was passed out, and she began to panic. Would he shoot him? She was terrified she'd hear the sound of a gunshot any moment. "Please, Vano, don't hurt him. Please don't hurt him!"

He came back in the doorway and pointed the gun at her. "You keep you're mouth shut or I will."

She nodded. "Okay, I swear. Just please don't hurt him."

"What do you care? You care more about that son-of-a-bitch from Brothers Ink than you do about your own family? Huh? He's my fucking competition. He's the enemy!"

"No, Vano, he's not your enemy. Please, just listen to me. You need to calm down. You're not thinking clearly."

He took another hit off his cigarette. "I'm thinking clearly, and I know exactly what I need to do.

He moved into the other room.

There was the sound of the metal against wood, desk across floor, and other sounds like maybe he was dragging Liam. She strained to hear. There was the sound of a drawer opening and closing and then the sound of another set of handcuffs closing around something. She couldn't imagine what he'd handcuffed Liam to.

"Vano! What are you doing? Just let us go, please."

Velvet suddenly remembered her cell phone in the pocket of the sundress. She pulled it out and opened the voice memo app, then set it on the floor beside her hip out of Vano's sight. Maybe she could get a recording of him confessing and give it to Sanders. Then this nightmare would all be over. "Vano?"

He reappeared in the doorway and ran a hand

through his hair. He was breathing hard. Apparently dragging Liam around was hard work. She noticed the cigarette was gone from his hand. In its place was the duffle bag. It looked fuller now, like maybe he'd taken stacks of cash from the safe and stuffed them inside. She met his eyes. "I know about the scam you were running."

"What scam? You don't know shit."

"Yes, I do. I overheard Skin and Weasel making the calls."

"When?"

"A while ago."

"Yeah, so?"

"You're taking money from old people! They've never been your mark before. Don't you have a conscience at all?"

"Crime is crime, little sister. You think all those years growing up Pops was really painting houses? He ran a home repair scam for years. You think he cared how many people he hurt? You think he thought twice about them when he got home to us? I rode with him on his last trip. He taught me all about it, how to do it, how to find a good mark. I learned well."

"And I found the heroin, Vano. Did Pops teach

you that, too? Are you dealing drugs now?"

That brought his chin up, and he snarled, "That ain't your business. And I'm smarter than Pops. I learned a thing or two in prison. There's easier ways of making money than driving all over the country in a van pretending to be a damn handyman."

"Who are you selling the heroin to, Vano?"

"That doesn't concern you."

"Are Skin and Weasel in on this? Maybe Skin is the real boss of you now." She knew this would get to him.

"That piece of shit ain't the boss of me. He ain't the boss of shit."

"You sure? He seems like he's got you under his thumb."

"Shut up."

"Who are you selling the heroin to, Vano?"

"Okay, fine. I'm leaving town anyway, so what do I care if you know. That was all Skin, okay? Does that make you feel better, little sister? No, your brother's not a big-time drug dealer."

"Are you on something, Vano? Are you a heroin addict now?"

"Fuck no! I've been taking some pills to stay awake, is all. It's hard to keep up with those guys. You have no idea, Vee."

"Vano, how did you get mixed up with them?"

"It was stupid, okay. I conned Skin. He figured it out and wanted his money back. I didn't have it anymore. I'd used it to open this place. That's why I had to steal your money. It was to pay him back. It wasn't enough. He wanted more. Then the next thing I knew I was laundering drug money for them. They cut me in for part of it. It was easy money, Velvet, and I didn't have to do a damn thing to get it. I don't know. It all just got out of control, and now I don't know how to get rid of them."

"Vano—" She was about to tell him about Skin and Weasel when he cut her off.

"I'm in over my head, but I'm done with that, do you hear, done! Take care, sister. You're my final payment to that asshole. He wants you so bad, maybe he'll forget I took all the money."

He disappeared down the hall as Velvet's mouth fell open. Her own brother would give her over to that disgusting ex-con? At that moment, she realized her brother didn't love anyone but himself, and all her delusions of family, and all her guilt about them shattered like a plate glass window under a wrecking ball.

She heard the door slam, and felt a tear roll down her cheek. She brushed it away; she couldn't think about her family anymore. She had the beginnings of a new family now, and a man who loved her. "Liam!"

She heard only silence.

She grabbed up her cell phone to call 911, but the battery had died. "No! Shit, shit, shit!"

She only hoped it still had some of the recording she'd tried to make. Vano had confessed to everything. She studied the room she was in. She'd bugged the office, but she hadn't bugged the restroom. Could the FBI hear her if she called out? Had they already been listening? Or had Vano or Skin found and destroyed the bugs? Maybe that's why Skin was so intent on finding her. She had to try anyway. "Sanders! Can you hear me? I'm handcuffed! Vano is escaping with the drugs and money! Liam is hurt. Come get us! Help!"

She kicked her foot. "Goddamn it." She realized coming here was a mistake. She'd gotten overconfident, and she'd been naïve if she thought it was all going to be so easy. She'd been stupid to think she could just come in and find evidence and everything would be over. Fat chance. It was never going to be that easy. She shouldn't have underestimated Vano.

She heard movement in the office and moaning.

"Liam? Liam, are you okay? I'm here, baby." There was more moaning. "Liam!"

"Mmm. Velvet? Where are you? Fuck, my head hurts. What happened?"

"Liam? I'm trapped in the bathroom."

She heard rattling. "What the hell? Baby? I'm cuffed to the radiator."

"Vano hit you over the head. He cuffed me in the bathroom. He took off with all the money. He's leaving town."

"Baby?"

"Yes?"

"Did he hurt you?"

"No, I'm okay. My cell phone battery died. I tried to record Vano. He confessed everything to me, Liam."

"That's great. Did you call the police?"

"I tried, but it died before I could. What about yours?"

There were more rustling sounds.

"My phone's gone. He must have taken it, or maybe it fell out of my pocket when I hit the floor."

"Can you see it?"

"No. I guess we're gonna be stuck here awhile. Anybody else have a key to the place?"

"I don't think Cooter or Finn have one. If Skin had one—"

"Yeah, that won't matter anymore."

"Maybe we can scream when the guys show up later. Maybe they'll hear us."

"Maybe."

There was silence.

"Liam? Liam?!"

"Yeah?"

"Are you okay? Keep talking so I know you haven't passed out again."

"What do you want to talk about, babe?"

"I don't know, but I'm starting to freak out."

"Maybe your buddy in the FBI will show up soon."

"Maybe."

"Too bad there's not a landline phone on this desk. I can't reach the desk, but I probably could have pulled the phone off it by the cord."

"Vano's too cheap. There's just the one up by the register."

"He left his cigarette burning in the ashtray."

Velvet frowned. Why would Liam mention that? "He did?"

"Yeah. Babe?"

"What's wrong?"

"There's all that flammable stuff up there and that cigarette is burning down. I think it could fall off the ashtray if it burns back far enough."

"Liam, you're scaring me."

"You sure you can't get free? Wiggle your tiny wrist out of those cuffs?"

She pulled tight on it, fear flooding her. If Liam was concerned enough to worry her like this, he had to think they were in real danger. "I'm trying, but I can't do it."

"I'm trying to find something to pick the lock on these cuffs."

"Liam, I'm scared."

"Baby, you remember the tattoo expo?"

"Yes, why?"

"You were so hot rolling around on that stage. Hottest woman I'd ever seen in my life."

"What are you doing?"

"Trying to get your mind on anything but where we are, Velvet."

"Do you think we're going to die here?"

"We're not going to die. We're going to get out of here."

She heard the sound of a boot scraping across the floor. "What are you doing?"

"I'm trying to reach the tattoo needle laying on the floor over by the desk. I can barely reach it. Fuck!"

"Liam?"

"If I can get it, maybe I can pick the lock on these cuffs with it."

She quietly waited, praying, and giving thanks for once that the shop was so dirty. There was a whooshing sound. "Liam, what was that sound?"

"The cigarette fell and rolled across the desk. The rubbing alcohol soaked wipes just flared up."

"Oh, my God."

"Baby, imagine we're somewhere you love. Where would you like to be right now?"

She could hear different sounds, one that might be him fiddling with the needle in the lock, one that might be the crackle of fire. "Liam, stop, I can't think about that now."

"Yeah, you can, baby. How about with the horses in the canyon? You loved that place, right? Imagine we're there."

A strong chemical smell reached her along with the scent of paper burning. "Liam, I smell smoke."

"Good. Maybe the smoke detectors will go off and someone will hear them. Hey, do you have a window in the bathroom?"

"Yes."

"Can you reach it?"

"It's got bars on the outside."

"Anything you can throw to break the glass? There aren't any windows in here or I'd do the same."

Velvet looked around. There was nothing. She glanced down at her phone. Maybe it was strong enough to break the glass. She'd probably be throwing away the evidence of Vano's confession, and with it maybe her chance at immunity from a twenty year sentence, but if she didn't they both might die in a fire. There was no question what she would do; she only hoped it would break the window. She paused with her hand in the air. "Wait. Will this make the fire flare up, I mean, the outside air source?"

"Baby, we need to get out of here. The stack of magazines is burning, and the ceiling tile is starting to blacken and melt."

"Oh, God, Liam. Can you pick the cuffs?"

"I'm trying, baby."

She hurled the phone at the window. The glass cracked but didn't break. She stomped her foot on the tile in frustration, and screamed on the top of her lungs as the smoke detectors went off. Thick black smoke rolled out of the office and drifted across the ceiling of the hallway.

"Liam! Liam! Help us! Help! Fire!"

Liam suddenly was in the door, he paused his hands on the frame as a coughing fit took hold of him. "B-baby."

He staggered to her, dropped to his knees, and tried to fiddle with her handcuff.

The smoke had made him woozy, and his eyes were watering. She coughed and covered her mouth and nose with the fabric of her dress. "Baby, cover your mouth."

He looked at her, trying to focus. "I have to get you free."

"Liam, look at me! Get the fire extinguisher! It's in the break room across the hall. Go. Quick."

He staggered to his feet, disappearing into the smoke.

She pulled on the cuff.

A moment later, she heard the extinguisher. It went on for about thirty seconds and then it sputtered out. Something clattered to the floor. "Liam!"

He appeared back in the doorway and paused to rest against the frame, hacking and coughing. Then he collapsed to the floor.

"Liam! Help us! Help!" Velvet screamed and screamed for help. Finally, she heard glass shatter from the front of the shop.

"Velvet?" It was Sanders.

"We're in here! Hurry!"

He appeared in the doorway, a blue windbreaker with FBI in bold yellow letters on and an ax in his hands. She saw some activity behind him as more agents rushed in, then she heard the sirens of a fire engine pull up outside.

"We've got a man down in here!" He stepped over Liam and moved to Velvet, dropping the ax to the floor. "Are you hurt?"

She shook her head. "I'm okay. Get Liam out; he needs oxygen!"

Two agents bent over him and dragged him toward the front of the building.

Velvet looked up at Sanders with tears in her eyes. "He has to be okay."

"He will be. Let's get you out of here." He reached in his pocket for keys, squatted down, and fumbled with the cuffs.

"Never thought I'd be happy to see you," she said, watching him.

The corner of his mouth lifted. "Mutual."

"It took you long enough."

"Sorry about that. We were busy chasing Vano."

"Did you catch him?"

"Yes, ma'am. Him, three bricks of heroin, and a shitload of cash."

"Not to mention the money in all those accounts he has."

"Right, we've frozen them already."

He unlocked the cuffs, and she drew her arm down, rubbing her wrist. She nodded to her phone on the floor. It lay face up, its screen shattered. "I recorded his confession on that, but I don't know if it saved it, the battery died, plus I just broke it."

He shoved it in his pocket. "If there's anything on it, our guys will be able to pull it off, don't worry."

"So, we almost died. Have I done enough to get that immunity?"

He nodded. "I think so, Ms. Jones. We got our man, with your help, of course." He pulled her to her feet, and she swayed. "You okay?"

"I'm fine. Just take me to Liam. Please."

"You got it, lady." He scooped her up in his arms and carried her out the front door.

A fireman was administering oxygen to Liam, who

was just coming around. When he saw Velvet, he ripped the mask off and started to move toward her. It took three firemen to hold him down.

Sanders carried Velvet to him and set her on the ground next to him. "Easy, big guy. She's fine."

They fell into each other's arms. Velvet clung to his neck, and Liam's arms went around her back, crushing her to him. She never wanted to let go. She wanted to stay here in his arms forever.

"I thought I lost you," they both murmured simultaneously, and the emotion of the situation overwhelmed them, and they broke into big smiles, their eyes sparkling with emotional relief.

"I love you, Velvet." Liam smoothed her hair back from her face, and she broke down in sobs. He crushed her to him. "Don't cry, baby. We made it."

CHAPTER THIRTY-TWO

"I love your new style," Liam murmured as he ran his fingers through her shorter hair. It was no longer jet black. It was now the color it had been when she'd first walked into his shop as a fifteen-year-old—her natural color, she'd told him. They were on his sofa, her head in his lap and her legs resting up on the back of the sofa.

She held up her finger. "Shush."

He smiled as she followed along with her finger on the page of the book she held in her hand, sounding out the words carefully. She paused on one of the longer words.

"Pra-pra… What's this word?"

"Sound it out."

She let out a huff of frustration. "I was."

"Practice."

"Practice," she repeated.

"Um hmm, practice. How about we *practice* what we were doing in the shower this morning," he teased, leaning down to kiss her forehead, his hand reaching toward the waistband of her jeans.

She smacked his hand away. "I'm reading."

Liam's phone went off. He dug it out of his pocket and looked at the screen. It was Jameson.

"Hello."

"Hey, what are you doing?"

"Not helping you move that heavy-ass piano, that's for sure."

"Ha ha. That's not why I'm calling, and yes you are—next Sunday."

"So, why are you calling?" Liam grinned down at Velvet who was frowning up at him, mouthing the word, *piano?*

"Is Velvet there?"

"Of course."

"Can the two of you come down to the shop?"

"Why?"

"Can you just come down? I'll tell you when you get here."

"Hmm, I don't know. Sounds suspicious."

"Just get your asses down here." Jameson hung up.

Liam pulled the phone from his ear. "Rude son-of-a-bitch."

"What's going on?"

"He wants us down at the shop."

"Why?"

"He wouldn't say."

She twisted and set her feet on the floor. "Let's go."

"No, he was rude. I say we stay home and have wild, crazy, monkey sex."

"Monkey sex? Ew."

"Wild, crazy, alpha-male, bondage sex?"

"Uh, let's go."

"What's in it for me?"

"There has to be something in it for you?"

"Uh, yeah."

"I'll buy you one of those fried doughnut things."

"They're called Spritzkuchen."

"You want one or not?"

"Fine. I'll go. But only because I'm hungry."

Ten minutes later, they strolled into the shop with a bakery box. The shop was closed, and no one was on the first floor, but the sound of a guitar drifted down from upstairs, so they headed up to Jameson's office.

Rory was sitting on the couch, his feet up on the coffee table, playing licks on his guitar. Jameson and Ryan Kelly were sitting in adjacent chairs.

"What's in the box?" Jameson asked.

Liam pulled it back a few inches. "Depends on why you wanted us down here. Nothin' for you, if I don't like the answer."

"You'll like the answer," Ryan said. He stood and extended his hand to Velvet. "Velvet, it's good to see you again."

She shook it. "Ryan, what brings you here?"

"You."

"Oh, really?" Liam asked. "Why's that?"

"Why don't you both sit down, and we'll talk."

Liam moved to the other side of the couch. When Velvet moved to sit between Rory and him, he pulled her onto his lap instead. His arms encircling her waist, he said, "So talk."

Ryan looked to them both. "The issue with the two of you on the cover did phenomenal sales. Only second to the cover we did with Jameson, and the best we've ever done with a couple on the cover."

"Really?" Velvet's face lit up, and Liam couldn't be happier for her. That kind of thing didn't matter to him, but he was happy to be a part of it if it made her this happy.

Ryan nodded. "The response to the article and

interview with you was overwhelming. Jameson told me you two are together now. The magazine wants to do another issue with the two of you as a couple, and I'm sure they'd love an article on how you found each other."

Liam rubbed his hand up Velvet's back, and she twisted, meeting his eyes. "I think I'd like to keep that story private, how about you, babe?"

She nodded.

"Well, you wouldn't have to share everything," Ryan jumped in, trying to persuade them. "Think about it. In the meantime, there was something else I wanted to talk to Velvet about."

"What's that?" Liam asked as she turned back to face the reporter.

"Did you like the article I wrote?"

"I did. Liam read it to me. You did a good job."

"I've found a publisher interested in your story. They've offered us a book deal, that is, if you want me, I'd love to be your co-author and tell your story."

"You talked about this, but I never really thought it would happen."

"They've made a good offer, which of course they would present to you officially, but I can tell you unofficially, it was a fifty thousand dollar advance."

Liam watched the expression on Velvet's face. It was enough money for the coffee shop she'd dreamed of. He squeezed her. "That's wonderful, baby."

She gave him a blank look. "I…I don't know. I'll have to think about it."

Liam frowned. "Why? What's to think about?"

"Liam, this wouldn't be a three page magazine article; they'd want enough to fill an entire book. I'd have to reveal things in much more detail. I just don't know if I'm ready. And with Vano's trial hanging over my head…"

Liam nodded. "Of course. No pressure. Whatever you want to do."

"I understand your concerns, Velvet. If you'd like we could work up a draft outline, just to see it all laid out. That might help you to decide if you'd want to proceed. I don't want to pressure you into anything either."

"Thank you. I suppose we could do that."

"Perhaps we can schedule some time next week?"

She nodded. "All right."

"Wonderful. I'll be in touch. Oh, and one other thing. The magazine was interested in shooting a calendar with you and Liam."

"Really?"

"I don't think you realize, you two are the "It Couple" in the tattoo world right now. You both should capitalize on that while you can."

"We'll let you know," Liam told him. He didn't want everything to overwhelm Velvet.

Ryan nodded, his gaze shifting between them. "They'll need to know on that by the end of the month, deadlines and all that. Well, I'll give you time to think it all over. I think you have some amazing opportunities in front of you. I'll be in touch." Ryan stood and shook their hands, then shook Jameson's. "Jameson, thank you for your time and for the use of your office." He turned to Velvet. "I look forward to hearing from you."

While Jameson walked Ryan out, Liam caught Velvet's face in his hand and turned her to meet his eyes. "That's some offer. What do you think?"

"I don't know. I'll have to think about it long and hard. I don't want to jeopardize what we have."

"And how would it jeopardize it?"

She shrugged. "It's a lot to put out there. My past, my family, the crimes they've committed… I just don't know."

Liam nodded. No way in hell was he going to push her into this; he didn't care how much it paid. He glanced down at his watch.

"You got someplace you have to be, brother?" Rory asked.

"Actually, I do."

Velvet frowned. "You do?"

"Yeah, I, uh, had something planned today, someplace I wanted to show you."

"What?"

"Let's take a walk, and I'll show you." They stood, and he turned and patted Rory's knee. "I like that riff. You got words to go with it?"

Rory put the guitar aside and stood. "Nah. I struggle with songwriting. Not my strong suit."

"Maybe you just haven't found the right topic yet. Dig deep, brother. I'm sure there are a bunch of great songs in there." He tapped Rory's chest with his fist.

"Thanks."

"See ya later."

Liam and Velvet exited the shop, and he drew her to the right. "This way."

"Where are we going?"

"It's a beautiful day, and it's only a short walk.

You'll see." They walked hand in hand through town. Liam glanced over at Velvet. "Do you like this town?"

She smiled brightly at him. "I love it. You're here."

"I mean the town itself."

"I love this area. Main Street has so many great shops and restaurants. It's really a happening area, especially with the street fairs and farmers market."

They walked two blocks and Liam stopped them on the corner. "We're here."

"What's here?" She looked around.

He nodded to the business on the corner. "This used to be Randall's Western Wear. Place has been here for thirty-seven years. Old man Randall died last year and his son has no interest in the business. They finally closed the doors last week."

"O-kay, and…?"

He pointed up to the sign in the multi-paned bay window. "Can you read that?"

She studied it. "Re-tail Sp-ace… I don't know those other words on the second line."

"It says *Retail Space Available For Lease*."

"For the coffee shop, you mean?"

He nodded, smiling. "It's a perfect location."

"Yes, but those are usually so expensive."

"Mr. O'Rourke?"

Liam turned to see the woman he'd been expecting. "Yes, ma'am."

"I hope I'm not late. I had a showing in Fruita this morning."

"Not at all. You're right on time. We just got here."

He caught the confused frown on Velvet's face.

"Velvet, this is Janet Parker. She's specializes in commercial real estate."

The woman extended her hand. "Pleased to meet you, Velvet. Liam's told me what you're looking for and I think this could fit the bill. It just became available and it's a hot property." She jangled some keys in the lock and swung the glass door open, flipping on the lights. "The place has only been vacant two days. You're the third showing I've had. If you like it, we should probably move fast. Locations on this part of Main Street never last long."

Liam and Velvet followed her inside.

"Being that it was a western wear store, its kind of rustic as you can see with wood planking for flooring and the stone fireplace on that wall. I think it has a certain sort of charm though especially with the bay window in front and the multi-paned glass." She looked at Velvet. "Do you think this would suit your needs? Is the space large enough for you?"

Velvet studied the space and nodded, her eyes glazing over.

Liam glanced over at Ms. Parker. "Could you give us a moment?"

"Of course. I'll be outside making some phone calls. Take as long as you need."

After she'd exited, the bell that still hung over the door jingling, Liam turned back to Velvet and pulled her to him. "Baby, what's wrong?"

She looked up at him and shook her head. "It's perfect."

"Then what's the problem?"

She shook her head, and then blew out a breath. "For my coffee shop to be successful, I have to have customers."

Liam frowned. "You will. The location is amazing and—"

She cut him off. "Liam, if I do the book, would people in town think differently of me? Would they ever let me put my past behind me? Would they ever accept me into the community? Because if they don't, how will my business ever succeed? And yet, I need the book money to make that dream come true, don't I? It's a catch-22, isn't it?"

"Velvet, you're worrying about things that haven't even happened yet."

"All right, let's talk about something that has already happened—the damage I've done to you and your family. Liam, maybe it would be best for everyone if I didn't stay in town."

"That's bullshit."

"Is it? What happens when everything about my brother's trial comes out? Maybe I'll never be accepted in this town after everything that's happened."

"And maybe you will be." He took her upper arms in his hands. "Velvet, you are not your brother, and no one is going to hold you accountable."

"I don't know. This is a big gamble."

"The biggest gamble I ever made in my life was going after you, and it pays off every day I am with you. I swear to you, this is going to work."

She studied him. "You seem so sure."

"I am sure. When something feels right you don't question it."

"I've always wanted to be accepted, to 'belong' in a community. I'm just worried that in this town I've got more to overcome than I would in another town."

"Velvet, it's not just about you anymore. I'm in this,

too."

"I realize that."

"Do you? I have family in this town. We have a business in this town. We have roots. I have every reason to want to stay here, but if you're telling me it's a choice between you and staying in Grand Junction, then I'll pack my bags and leave it all to be with you. Because I love you, I would do that. I guess I'm hoping you won't make me make that choice."

"I would never want to make you leave your home and family and work."

"So what are you saying? Because whatever we do, we're doing it together. I love you, Velvet."

"I love you, too, Liam."

"Then say yes, to me, to Grand Junction, and to making all your dreams come true—together."

But still she worried that she was going to be a bad influence in the eyes of the town, and she wasn't sure she could do that to Liam and his business. She'd always wanted to be accepted by the town, not shunned.

"I'm standing here, willing to risk it all for you. You have to be willing to take that risk with me, Velvet. Together we can do anything. Because our love is worth any risk we have to take."

"I love that you make me feel like anything is possible."

"Because it is possible, as long as we've got love, and each other, anything we want is possible. So let's sign the lease and walk down the street to the jewelry store and put a ring on your finger."

She burst out in happy tears and hugged him. "Yes, yes, I want all those things."

EPILOGUE

Liam –

I swung the ax up and brought it down with driving force, the handle gliding through my palms until the blade sunk deep into the bark of the spruce tree. I yanked it out with a jerk, the muscles in my arms flexing. A couple more swings, and the tree toppled over. Wiping the sweat from my brow with the back of my glove, I bent and grabbed the trunk and dragged it down to where I'd parked my truck and hefted the tree into the bed. We'd had a dusting of snow last night, just enough to leave a trail of my boot prints.

Jumping in the cab, I pulled my buckskin gloves off and started the engine, imagining the smile I hoped the tree would put on Velvet's face when she saw it. She'd hinted around about it, but I'd been vague and noncommittal. I wanted it to be a surprise.

I drove into town. Lights were already strung

across Main Street and had been since Thanksgiving. Every tree along the sidewalk was lit. I loved when the town decorated. It looked beautiful at night, like driving through a tunnel of lights.

I parked in front of *Coffee on the Corner* and hopped out. Dropping the tailgate, I grabbed the tree. It slid across the bed liner without a single dropped needle. That was the awesomeness of a fresh cut tree, that and the fabulous scent.

The tree was eight feet and I had to wrangle it in the front door, but with the help of a customer who held the door for me, I managed. The ceilings inside were twelve feet high and I knew she'd need a tree big enough to fill the space.

I stopped just inside the door, standing the tree up with a thunk.

Velvet had just finished waiting on a customer, and when she saw me, or maybe my gift, her face lit up. She ran around the counter, and I caught her to me as she threw her arms around my neck. "You brought me a tree!"

"You dropped enough hints. Did you think I was dense?"

She pulled back and kissed my mouth. "Of course not." Her eyes swept over it. "It's gorgeous, and it smells so good."

"Where do you want it? In the front bay window or back by the fireplace?"

She bit her lip. "I think by the fireplace. That way it's near the children's reading corner. I don't want to block the window or have to rearrange the tables. People love sitting near the bay windows and people watching."

"You got it, babe." I carried the tree to the back and leaned it against the wall. Then I went to the truck and carried in the big stand. When I had it all set up, Velvet came and admired it.

"It's perfect, Liam."

"Glad you like it." I pulled her against my hip and kissed the tip of her nose. "The place looks great. You really went all out decorating. I suppose I shouldn't be surprised, considering how you had the place fixed up for Halloween."

"Well, it was my opening month, and I wanted this place to be a place that kids wanted to visit."

I glanced around. True to her word, she'd put in a children's reading corner with a big colorful rug and several soft beanbag chairs. The walls were lined with shelves full of children's books. There were also several cozy stuffed chairs for parents to sit and read to the younger ones. "Well, you managed that."

On Halloween she'd outdone herself with decorations, turning the shop into something right out of Harry Potter. Then she'd had a Halloween party with free apple cider and cookies for children, inviting them to come down in their costumes for special prizes. It had been a huge hit with not only the kids, but the parents as well, who were always looking for something fun to do with the little ones. The community had looked past her tattoos and accepted her wholeheartedly.

The coffee shop was cheerfully decorated and very inviting and soon became a real gathering place. Velvet was in her element.

And now as I looked around at what she'd done for the children in decorating for Christmas, I knew this place was going to be somewhere they remembered from their childhood long after they'd grown up.

She had a toy train running around the shop up on shelving that she'd had my brothers and I install when we remodeled the place for her. She wouldn't tell me what it was for, but had insisted on it. It was a big hit with the kids.

There were decorations everywhere, Santa figures

and snowmen and elves galore. Combine that with the smell of her fabulous coffee drinks and the baked goods she sold, and the place was a hit.

The bay windows were frosted with fake snow, and a sandwich board sign out on the sidewalk noted the coffee of the day. Today's was Peppermint Swirl.

A child ran up to us and tugged on her apron. "Miss Velvet, I can't reach the mailbox slot to drop my letter to Santa."

She squatted down and looked at the letter the child had written at the small round table in the children's reading corner. Velvet had asked me to create a mailbox on a stand that said North Pole on it so the children could mail their letters.

"Well, come with me. I'll help you." She took the little girl with her bouncing blonde ringlets and walked her over to the box. "We need to fold it and put it in an envelope so it fits."

I watched my angel as she helped the child mail her letter. My heart was full to bursting, seeing the joy on her face. My Velvet had longed to be accepted in the community. She'd achieved that and more. She wasn't just accepted, she was loved.

Pam from the animal shelter walked over to

me. Her eyes on Velvet, she leaned close. "Everyone loves her, Liam. The children, their parents, the whole town… You should be proud."

"I am."

"You look happy."

I nodded. "You don't have to look too far to see the reason why."

She smiled and patted my cheek. "We're having a holiday adoption fair at the shelter next weekend. You'll be there?"

I pulled her against my side for a hug. "You know I will."

"I've got a cute little tabby cat that just came in. I think it would look really cute curled up in front of that fireplace. She could be the coffee shop cat."

I grinned. "Oh, Lord. You show her to Velvet, we'll be taking it home for sure."

"That's the plan. I'll see you later."

Pam walked toward the front door, and my eyes shifted to Velvet. She was so good with the kids that came in here, always squatting down to their level and talking to them, always that big smile on her face. The funny thing about kids, they didn't see the tattoos; they saw her, recognizing innately the good person she was underneath. I knew someday she'd make a wonderful mother.

A few minutes later she returned to my side.

She went up on her toes and kissed my lips. "Thank you for my tree."

I caught the back of her head and brought her in for longer kiss. I released her, and she made a purring sound. "That's just a preview of what you're going to get when you get home tonight."

She gave me a saucy wink that promised all kinds of things. "Oh, honey, you have no idea."

"Hmm, I may have to leave the shop early tonight."

She smiled up at me and tucked a folded piece of paper into my flannel shirt pocket and patted her hand over the pocket. The diamond ring she'd picked out at the jewelry store down the street, sparkled. We'd gotten married outside at the farm, and although I wanted to give her a big wedding, she'd wanted it simple. I loved her, and I'd give her anything she wanted, so we'd kept it simple with just my immediate family.

I glanced down and frowned. "What's that? Another honey-do list?"

"Nope. Just a little note for you to read later."

I started to pull it from my pocket, but she

stopped me, insisting, "Later."

I noticed the paper she'd written it on was the cute stationary she'd put out on the kid's table for them to write their letters to Santa. Apparently she'd just written it a few moments ago.

She'd been working hard the last few months learning to read and write, and I was so proud of her. I helped her whenever I could. I knew the fact that she'd spent her life illiterate was especially painful for her and that was one of the reasons she was so intent on having the children's reading corner at the coffee shop. She wanted to provide easy access to books in a place that was fun for both parents and kids to come and hangout.

"All right, weirdo, I'll read it later."

"Get out of here. I have to get back to work."

"Yes you do. Go make us some money."

"Love you."

"Love you, too, babe."

I walked out to my truck and got behind the wheel. I pulled out onto the street, but I didn't make it farther than the red light before I dug the note from my pocket and read it.

Liam –

When I was a girl, I always hoped that one day someone

would walk into my life and get it right where everyone else got it wrong.

I hoped that one day I'd finally meet someone who wanted to help me grow in life, someone I could finally trust with everything.

And I hoped that one day I'd have my best friend, my biggest supporter, and my lover all wrapped up in one person.

That day arrived the day I met you.

I love you, Liam, with all my heart.

– Velvet

My eyes glazed over as I stared down at the words. Her handwriting was still childish and inexperienced, but I would treasure this note all the rest of my days.

A car horn blared behind me, and I glanced up to see the light had changed to green. My boot slipped off the brake pedal and I gave the old truck some gas. I looked around my town; joy soaring through my veins, truly happy with a feeling of belonging that I had been missing for a long time. Everything in my life was finally settling perfectly into place.

Velvet –

That night, when Liam got home from work, I walked him into our bedroom with my hands over his eyes, hoping he'd love the surprise I'd had made for him. I'd been nervous all day for him to see it.

There up on the wall above our bed I'd framed the photo Aaron had snapped of me that day at the expo in LA. I was in the pose Liam had talked about, laying on the bed with my legs in the air looking back at the camera.

"You bought a white fur rug?" Liam guessed, teasing me, my hands still tight over his eyes.

"Nope."

"Good, because I already got one on order."

Ignoring his reply, I pulled my hands away and watched his face, holding my breath for his reaction, hoping he'd like my gift.

A big grin formed on his face as he took it in. "There's my girl."

He hooked his arm around my neck and pulled me to him. I had to ask. "Do you like it? I can take it down. Maybe it's too much."

"I love it, and you're not touching it."

"Liam, you know, I'm not the girl in that picture

anymore. That girl was a façade, a character, a persona I made up to cope with what I had become. She was a way to save myself."

He turned me to him. "And now you're saved."

"Yes."

He pulled my skimpy tank top over my head, leaving me standing in only my silk pajama shorts. His eyes moved over me, and I stood, content to let him take my body in.

"I can never get my fill of you, sweetness."

The man could turn me on with just a look, especially when his eyes darkened like they did now.

"I'm glad you let me put some new ink on you." He reached up and brushed the back of his fingers down the skin along my ribs. I'd picked out the wording and Liam had designed the swirling pattern that was intricate filigree twining down my curves.

It read, *I don't need you to save me – I just need you to stand beside me while I save myself.*

He tipped my head back with a finger under my chin, and I was lost in his warm brown eyes. He nodded to the portrait on the wall. "Velvet, I get what you just said, every word. But, baby, to me, a part of you will always be that sexy woman in that picture—the hottest woman I've ever seen. And I love that pose; it reminds me of how later that same night I had you for the very first time, and it was everything I ever dreamed. I married that girl, and she sleeps in my bed every night, and that makes me the luckiest man on the planet."

"Oh, Liam, you're going to make me cry."

"I'll love you forever, Velvet."

"Promise?" And then he did the one thing that had my heart melting and always would. He made an X over his chest.

"Cross my heart, baby-girl."

If you liked LIAM, please post a review on Amazon.

PREVIEW OF RORY

He was a total stranger, just a one-night stand, but for some reason she'd felt she could open up to him and pour out her most intimate experiences. The night they shared was magical, but they were headed in two different directions like two ships passing in the night. Or in this case, two Harleys passing in the night.

What do you do when someone writes a song about your most private feelings and experiences?

What do you do when you hear it on the radio for the first time?

What do you do when that song is climbing the charts, and the man who stole your life story is suddenly rock's hottest new artist?

What do you do when you find out you're having his baby?

ALSO BY NICOLE JAMES:

The Evil Dead MC Series:

OUTLAW: An Evil Dead MC Story

CRASH: An Evil Dead MC Story

SHADES: An Evil Dead MC Story

WOLF: An Evil Dead MC Story

GHOST: An Evil Dead MC Story

BLOOD: An Evil Dead MC Story

RED DOG: An Evil Dead MC Novella

UNDERTAKER: An Evil Dead MC Story

JOKER: An Evil Dead MC Story

The Brothers Ink Series:

JAMESON

MAXWELL

LIAM

Coming soon… RORY

Romantic Suspense:

RUBY FALLS